Always My Comfort

THE DEXTER BROTHER
BOOK FOUR

TAYLOR JADE

To my mom, for always believing in me.

Prologue

JAXON

10 Years Ago

"Touchdown! Ladies and gents, did you see that? Jaxon Dexter scored the first touchdown of the game, following right in the footsteps of his brothers! You better keep your eye on him, scouts! Football runs in his veins."

The crowd screamed, waving cowbells in the air, their hoots and hollers echoing around the small field. My teammates tackled me, and the turf scratched my skin, but I couldn't feel it. Not with their loud voices booming with praise.

The cheerleaders were waving their poms and cheering, all of them screaming my name.

At this moment, I was the king.

I was Jaxon Dexter, the younger brother of Archer, Dante, and Gage Dexter, all known as royalty on this field. I had a legacy to live up to, and I hated it.

"Dexter! Dexter! Dexter!" my teammates screamed, helping me to my feet. I stole a look into the crowd at the men who would decide if I would live the same legacy as my brothers—the scouts.

Archer, my oldest brother of four years, had gotten a full ride to a school with one of the best football programs. Just as he was about to hit NFL status, he sustained an injury, ending his football career.

Dante, older than me by three years, had followed in his footsteps, but he had made the league. His name held power and stature, a god I had to somehow live up to.

And then, there was Gage. Only two years separated us, but sometimes, it felt like a lifetime with how strained our relationship was at times. He also graduated with a full ride to college because of his talent, but he hated the game just like me, and he was the first Dexter to quit football.

And I was going to be the second.

Our dad had wanted us all to be in the league. He taught us the rules of the game before we even started elementary school. Archer had followed along his path, the perfect prodigal son... until he wasn't. And Dad was so bitterly disappointed.

Mom had been the soft place to fall when Dad yelled at us for not running fast enough or throwing far enough. She was there with fresh lemonade and a smile so big that everything else melted away.

Dante attempted to please Dad. He had made it to the league; his name was always on the tips of everyone's tongues in town. Dad was proud. Dante was now the favorite son, while Archer hid away in his room, denying seeing any of us and refusing help. My oldest brother had lost all hope.

The sport we had been groomed to love was something we were all starting to hate. Gage hated the game when he graduated from high school two years ago. He tried to keep it hidden from Arch and Dante, but I knew. We'd often talk about the possibility of a different life.

A row above the scouts sat my father. He was wearing a shirt with my jersey number on it, a big grin cracking his weathered face. This made him happy.

Us following in his footsteps made him smile like nothing I

had ever seen before, and I wanted nothing more than to make him proud of me, just like he was of my older brothers.

I scored another touchdown by the end of the second quarter, and then, it was finally halftime. Dad was waiting for me outside the locker room, arms crossed over his chest, lips curled into a grin.

"You did good, son." He clapped his hand onto my shoulder pads and yanked me in for a hug.

"Thanks, Dad." I swept my wet hair off my forehead and looked out back toward the bright lights.

"Go refuel. The scouts are impressed. You should see an offer from them soon. Try to score another one before the game ends." I nodded and headed into the locker room, where the water boy handed me a Gatorade.

"Good job out there, Dexter. You might just be the best Dexter I've had on my field," Coach complimented. Red crept up my neck. Archer had been a king on the field; I couldn't imagine throwing him off his throne, nor did I want to. Football had been everything to him, and now, it was gone. "Keep up the good work and bring us to the championships!" He slapped my back and then moved on to the next player.

I sat alone for the next few minutes, trying to regroup my thoughts. My phone buzzed on the bench next to me, and Archer's face flashed on the screen.

I put the cold phone to my sticky face. "Surprised to hear from you," I muttered, looking at my grass-stained cleats.

"You're doin' a good job out there, but your head isn't in it. You could be better. I know you, Jax. You're better than Dante and I put together."

Arch had always known the inner workings of my mind before even I did. But voicing my thoughts on a game that was too important to my family felt damn near impossible.

"Just tired Arch. Tired of carryin' the whole team," I whispered so none of the other guys could hear me.

"You just need to impress the scouts. Doesn't matter if the

3

team loses. So long as you look good and score points, they'll be interested."

"Because of Dante, I know. Dad briefed me before the game. Everyone is watchin' me because of him." I chugged the bottle of Gatorade and tossed the empty bottle to the floor.

"Not because of Dante. Cause of you. You're a damn good player, brother."

"How's the leg?" I changed the subject because I knew it pissed him off to talk about his injury. There was one thing all us Dexter boys had in common. We hated showing any weakness.

"I didn't call to talk about me," came his gruff response.

"Off the phone, Dexter. Time to get back on the field and kick some ass!" Coach shouted from the front of the locker room. The entire team turned to look at me. I quickly ended the call without a goodbye.

Following my teammates out onto the field, my name was a cheer across the stands as I waved. Dad shot me a thumbs up as he settled back into his seat. It was going to be hard to give this up. Once he found out I planned on quitting, he would never look at me the same way again.

I scored another two touchdowns. My name was screamed from every corner of the field as we won the game. My teammates lifted me into the air, and Coach yelled his excitement.

"Hell yes, Dexter! That's what I'm talkin' about!"

"Jaxon! Jaxon! Jaxon!"

"Dexter, you're a beast!"

My eyes found Dad's, who was looking nervously at the scouts, but he had nothing to worry about. They were grinning, jotting down notes on their clipboards. I was in. I played the way Arch said I could.

God-given talent, I had been told my whole life, but really, it was years of practice.

My team finally put me down on my feet, and I reached for the Gatorade the water boy was passing me. After chugging the bottle,

4

I threw it in the trash and walked over to Dad, who was hanging by the edge of the field, the bright lights shining down on the biggest grin I had ever seen him wear.

"You did good, Jax. Wish your brothers could have seen this game. They would've been proud." He slung an arm around my shoulders, pulling me closer to him. "Those scouts—they were damn speechless."

The scouts he was talking about were walking over to us now, all three of them closing the space between us and the grandstands quickly.

"Jaxon, that was quite the game," one of them said, adjusting the peak of his hat on his balding head. Dad pushed me forward, and I stumbled over my cleats, hand outstretched like I had been taught.

"Thank you, sir. Been playing with my brothers since before I could walk." I cracked the joke, and the three of them chuckled.

"The Dexter name is well known in the league. It was an unfortunate loss when Archer tore his ACL, but Dante seems to be making up for it."

Internally, I cringed. Dante wasn't making up for anything. He was playing the sport he loved to the best of his ability to make Dad proud.

"He's the reason I play. Archer and I used to play on this field together." I nodded toward the field behind us.

As much as I hated the sport, some of my best memories were on this field with my brothers. In my first year of high school, we were all on the team together, and now, we were all in different stages of our lives.

"We'll be keeping an eye on you for the rest of the season. Hopefully, you'll consider playing for us in college." The scout handed me a business card with the team logo and his name. I nodded and accepted the card.

This was an offer.

This was a chance to make Dad happy.

This was my chance out of this town, where I wouldn't be Jaxon Dexter, the little brother of Archer, Dante, and Gage Dexter.

"Thank you, sir; I'd be honored." Shaking hands with the scout, I sealed my fate.

CHAPTER 1

Logan

RAIN PELTED AGAINST THE ROOF OF MY GYNECOLOGIST'S office. I tapped my sneaker against the tile flooring and scrolled through my Instagram feed tirelessly, liking posts of people I had known in high school and college. Every smiling engagement announcement or baby gender reveal was another reminder of how far away I was from where I planned to be at twenty-six.

A nurse stuck her head in the room, jarring me from my fantasies. "Doc will be a few more minutes, hun. Hang tight." She closed the door quietly before I could say anything, and I turned back to my phone.

I had plans for when I was twenty-six. I wanted to be married with two kids and a dog. At least, that was my ten-year goal from when I was sixteen. The same goal I had told my best friend, Scarlet, who had laughed at me and swore she would never marry before thirty.

Ironic since she tied the knot last summer, and I had stood at her side as her maid of honor, silently questioning how our lives had been reversed.

There was a soft knock on the door, and then my doctor finally walked in. Dr. Williams smiled at me, her hair pulled back

7

into a ponytail that swished with each calculated step she took into the small room.

"How are you, Logan?" She was only a few years older than me, but her voice was hoarse from years of smoking. The stale scent of nicotine filled the space, and I fought the cough building in my chest.

Clearing my throat, I licked my dry lips and smiled at her. "Never been better." The same lie I repeated every year slipped easily from my lips. There was no point in telling this woman, who I only saw once a year, that I was downright miserable.

"So, you're here for your annual exam and prescription renewal?" She wasn't looking at me but instead at the clipboard of my charts, I presumed.

"Yes, although, I don't see a point of the birth control now." I sighed, and she looked up, brows drawing.

"Are you planning on trying with, uh, what's his name again?" She tried to recall my ex's name, and I cringed. We'd spoken extensively about him last time I was here. I had told everyone and anyone who was willing to listen about my Major League Baseball-playing boyfriend. I had told Dr. Williams how I knew he was going to propose soon and how we were going to make the prettiest babies.

Look where that got me.

"We broke up a few months ago actually, and I don't see any men in my future." I tried to laugh it off, but my voice was strained. I crossed my arms over my chest. She nodded and looked back at her chart and then at me, not voicing the question in her hollow eyes.

"Ms. Shaw, you were right about the birth control. I can't renew the prescription." She wrote something down and then put the clipboard down and focused on me.

"And why not? I was only joking." She plastered on a smile that I didn't like. One that I knew was going to bring bad news.

"Because you're three months pregnant."

"No, no, no." I shook my head so hard, my head hurt. "You must have my results mixed up with someone else's." I stood and paced the room. My heart was beating loudly in my ears, making it hard to listen to Dr. Williams as she told me all about the wonderful news. I reached for the hand tightening around my throat and came up empty.

I had been fighting anxiety attacks for a few weeks now and knew the signs.

This is not happening.

It isn't possible.

"You haven't had any symptoms?" she questioned, remaining calm, while my mind was running haywire.

I pulled at the chain around my neck, at the silver cross my mom had given me for my eighteenth birthday. The one that usually kept me calm. *The only piece I had left of her.*

It didn't ease my nerves, but fidgeting with a piece of her eased my racing heart just a little, just enough that I could think clearly without the darkness clouding my judgment.

"No, I haven't even had sex in months! I mean, shit, I haven't even missed a pill." I started recounting the last couple of months.

Richard and I broke up four months ago. We hadn't been intimate in months. The relationship had been fizzling out for longer than I cared to admit, but he was always away from home. Playing away games in other states, late-night practices, and extra time at the gym.

There wasn't any time for us.

He didn't make time for me. Baseball was more important. It was his life. Hence our breakup.

"When was the last time you were intimate with your ex?"

"Nine months ago on New Year's Eve." It had been the worst sex of my life. He was drunk, and I wished I was, too. More than that I wished I had been strong enough to say no because, as usual, he got what he wanted and fell asleep while I was left there staring

9

at the ceiling, wondering if this was what the rest of my life would be like.

"Anyone else? It's not his baby, Logan," she gently reminded me, and I wracked my brain, trying to remember someone else.

Shit.

"It's Jaxon Dexter's," I whispered. He'd been in the bar that night.

The night I came home to another girl in Richard's bed and fled to the local bar, where Jaxon and his team were celebrating their win against Richard's team. My perfect boyfriend had been just like all the other players. A no-good, piece of shit.

Mom would have been so disappointed if she could see me now. Cheated on by a baseball player and pregnant with another one's child.

She always told me to stay away from them. I should have listened. I didn't want to be a cleat chaser, yet here I was.

The same night Richard locked me out of his apartment and I missed two days of my prescription while I licked my wounds and found the courage to go in there while he was at practice.

Two whole days. After a one-night stand with the sexiest man I had ever seen.

"But we used a condom," I sputtered, choking on the realization that there was a baby growing inside of my very flat stomach.

"They aren't always effective, but that's beside the point. I would like to do an ultrasound, and then get you a list of prenatal vitamins you need to begin immediately."

"This is all too fast; I'm not even married! This goes against my ten-year plan!" I screamed, shoving my distressed hands through my hair.

"Is there someone you want to call? Maybe your best friend?" Scarlet was the last person I wanted to call. She would only make fun of me for having hot sex with a stranger and then getting knocked up.

The person I wanted to call was unreachable. My mom.

"No. I just need a minute. This is all very alarming." She stood, nodding her head in understanding.

"I'm going to grab some pamphlets about what to expect and tell a nurse to come help you get prepped for the ultrasound so we can see the baby." She squeezed my hand and stepped out of the room, closing the door behind her.

I dropped into the plastic chair, covering my face with my hands. The first tear rolled down my cheek.

This isn't happening.

Slapping my hot cheeks, I prayed that I was going to wake up from this nightmare, but instead, there was only another knock on the door, and the same nurse from earlier came in.

"Alright, honey. Let's get you prepared for this ultrasound."

This had to be a dream.

This couldn't be real.

Twenty minutes later, after hearing my baby's heartbeat and seeing the very tiny, very real baby in my stomach, I was overcome with emotion—sadness, happiness, distress. I didn't know how I made it back to my car, but I was sitting there, tears streaming down my cheeks, a list of vitamins to take and a handful of pamphlets crumpled in my fist.

Holding my phone to my ear with a shaky hand, I waited for Scarlet to answer.

"What's up, bestie?" Her voice drew out the sob I'd been struggling to contain. "Oh, no, today was your doctor's appointment. Is everything okay? What's wrong?"

"I'm pregnant, Scar. I'm pregnant," I cried into the phone, throwing the papers on the passenger seat and picking up the black and white pictures of my baby.

My baby.

Something clattered to the ground, and Scarlet sighed. "Well, fuck. That wasn't part of the plan. Does Richard know?"

"It's not his," I whimpered, closing my eyes.

"No! You've been sleeping around? My best friend? Girl, who

are you, and what have you done with my boring best friend?" She giggled like I was the brunt of some hilarious joke, which made anger replace my sadness.

"This isn't a freaking joke, Scar. I'm pregnant from a one-night stand. A god damn one-night stand. Did you hear me? In case you didn't—a one-night stand!"

"Yes, I heard you. Now, who the hell knocked you up, buttercup? Please tell me he's cute. I want my god-baby to be cute. I'm sure he or she will be, but you know it doesn't hurt for the father to be good-looking." She was rambling like she always did, and usually, I'd play along, but I couldn't because none of this was funny.

"Jaxon Dexter." I hit my head on the steering wheel. "Jaxon freaking Dexter is the man I slept with."

"The pitcher for the Braves?" she asked.

"The one and only."

"Thank God! He's got one fine ass. I mean, seriously, have you seen it?" Rolling my eyes, I prayed for the strength to not strangle my best friend when I saw her later. "Wait—of course, you've seen it. Was it firm?"

"Scarlet!" She sighed.

"Okay, what do you want to do?"

"I have to tell him, right?" I sat up and glanced at the picture again. My baby that was the product of one of the worst nights of my life.

"Only if you want to."

"What do you think my mom would say?" She was going to miss this. Like she had missed all the milestones I'd had since cancer took her away from me.

"She wouldn't have cared as long as you were happy."

"She didn't want me to be a cleat chaser either," I reminded her.

"You aren't a cleat chaser. Seriously, Logan, you need to stop thinking so low of yourself. If I wasn't married, I'd have totally slept with Jaxon Dexter if he was offering. Speaking of, you need to tell me that story. How far long along are you?"

"Three months."

"Holy shit! And you didn't know the whole time? Didn't you notice you haven't had three periods?"

"It's always been irregular; I had no idea. I'm still in shock. I didn't believe the doctor until I saw the baby on the ultrasound. Oh, God, Scar—there's a very tiny baby inside me."

"It's going to be okay. Whatever you decide, I'm here. I'm going to be an aunt, Mattie!" she screamed at her husband, whose deep voice rumbled in the background of the call.

This isn't happening.

CHAPTER 2

Jaxon

The sticky summer air clung to my skin as I pushed myself to run harder, faster. I needed to be the best; I had to be for them to choose me since I'm so late in the game. I had to prove that I was worthy before it was too late.

The Georgia sun beat down on my face. Sweat rolled down my face and along my neck until it reached the hem of the shirt I was wearing. I'd regretted wearing it the moment I stepped outside. But I had to protect my skin. I spent enough time in the sun to know the harm it could cause.

Tonight was my last chance to get recruited. The rosters were full for most of the bigger teams, but Coach had promised me the recruiters would be there tonight. He swore I had potential. 'Natural talent,' he called it.

God, I hoped he was right.

I wanted this.

I could taste it.

I just had to be the best.

Running along the trail, I spotted my best friend waiting for me, leaning against a tree trunk. A baseball cap covered his head, the logo of the Tampa Bay Rays gleaming in the sunlight. Sunglasses hid his eyes as he stood upright, his arms crossed over his broad chest, grinning.

"You do know killing yourself before the game tonight won't help you get recruited, right?" Luke cracked a joke as I slowed to a jog, and he joined me, easily keeping pace.

We'd been running trails for the last year together before a big game. It was how we had become friends—through our love of letting off steam.

"I know that, but I have to get rid of the nerves somehow, and this does the trick," I grunted, catching his nod out of the corner of my eye. I knew he understood. Probably the only person who did.

He'd been a wreck a few months ago when he was offered a spot on two different teams, so we did a lot of running together. It helped him think, and I was there when he finally decided, and now, he was here for me.

"I hear from the grapevine that the Marlins are looking for a pitcher," he suggested. There had been talk of him being drafted to their team, so he had started to hang with some of the younger players, working his way in.

"I've had my eye on the Braves, to be closer to home. With my brothers settling down and starting families, I want to be involved, especially with my nieces and nephews." He already knew this, but it didn't stop him from cracking a joke.

"You thinking about settling down already? Isn't it too soon for the girl, house, dog, and kids?" He knew I wasn't interested in any of that. Hell, none of the guys on the team were thinking about marriage or kids.

I bumped my shoulder with his, and he nearly ended up in the bushes. But his laughter echoed around us.

"Melanie got you thinking about marriage again, buddy?" He snorted at my question about his girlfriend, the girl he'd been dating since high school.

"Look, I know she's the one. Doesn't mean we're even talking about marriage or any of that crap." He'd always been defensive about her. The entire team loved his girlfriend. Hell, she had been our biggest fan for a long time and took care of all of us.

"But you've thought about it?" I asked, slowing to take a drink from the water fountain we were nearing.

He leaned against the fountain as I bent to take a long gulp. He stared at the sky, searching for his answer, but I had three older brothers who had fallen for women. I knew what it looked like, and my best friend was a goner.

"Luke?" I stood, wiping away the sweat from my forehead.

He wiped a hand down his face and sighed, looking ten years older in just one minute. "We had a pregnancy scare a few nights ago," he mumbled, looking at me and then back at the trail. "And you know the worst part?"

I waited for him to keep talking. He loved Melanie more than his next breath, not that he'd ever admit it out loud, but he wasn't ready for kids, and neither was she.

"I got fucking excited, man. The thought of her pregnant with my kid... It just made sense in my head. For a whole hour, I saw the future. I saw the house, the dog, and the kids, and I was okay with it."

"But she isn't pregnant?" I questioned.

"Nah, just late. She forgot her doctor changed her to a new birth control." We resumed our jog, nodding at the other joggers as we passed them.

"How was she?" I asked when we stopped at our hotel building thirty minutes later.

"Devastated. Relieved. Fuck, I don't know. She locked herself in the guest bedroom and wouldn't come out. I still haven't spoken to her today," he said as we head into the lobby, cold air hitting us immediately.

"You've got an hour until Coach wants us at the field. Go on and call her. Tell her how much you love her, and it'll be okay.

Girls just want to know you feel the same." He raised his brow at me, and I knew immediately I was going to regret my advice.

"When did you become an expert?" We stepped into the elevator, and he pressed the button for our floors.

"Two sisters-in-law, man. Women talk; I listen."

"Right. Well, I'll see you in an hour. Go shower. You stink. And relax that arm or you won't be any good tonight." He clapped me on the shoulder and exited the elevator with a salute.

My older brothers had found their path. They weren't fumbling, getting lost, and turning back to find their way anymore.

I wanted to be like them. I was tired of stumbling in the dark, tripping over metaphorical roots and other obstacles. I was tired of playing a game I hated, tired of living up to everyone's expectations of who I was supposed to be.

Football had been everything.

Had been.

When Arch tore his ACL and was the first one of us to give up the game, I waited to see Dad's reaction, but he had none—just pure disappointment. Everyone was more worried about if Archer would be able to find his way. And then, the girl he had loved since he was a child came back to Honey Magnolia to settle her parents' estate. Suddenly, nobody, even Dad, seemed to care about the career Archer had lost. All they cared about was the love story between Archer and his now wife, Kenna.

Dante made it. He made the big league and even got close to playing in a Superbowl, but then, he gave it up. I watched Dad, saw his disappointment, but Dante was tired of the parties. He wanted the life Archer and Kenna were living. He wanted to settle down and start a family. The playboy of the family was tired of playing the field. And then, like all good things happen, the girl he'd been smitten with in high school ran back home, escaping her abusive husband. It was fate that he decided to come home that day.

Gage surprised us all when he quit football without telling a soul and dropped out of college to become a paramedic of all things. Then, just like our two brothers, he fell in love with his childhood friend.

I hadn't outright told any of them just how much I hated football. Archer knew I took up baseball in the off-season to keep fit, but he didn't know just how hard I fell for the sport. Standing there on the mound in the center of the field, preparing myself to pitch a strike...

The chaos in my mind finally fell to silence. The weight of everyone's approval disappeared. All that mattered was me, the ball, and the other player. With time, I had mastered my position, just like I had in football.

And over time, I had caught the eye of a few recruiters and cleat chasers.

The cleat chasers were like any young, naïve girl—chasing a guy, hoping to catch his eye for a chance at his fame. I had fallen for the trap once, and as soon as she started asking for money, I sent her packing and ignored all the other girls who wore my jersey number and screamed my name.

I wasn't looking for someone to settle down with. I wasn't looking for a quick tumble in the sheets either.

I was only focused on my path.

CHAPTER 3

Logan

Nose tucked into a book, knees pulled up to my chest, and glasses sliding down my nose, I curled into myself on the couch as the girl finally succumbed to her feelings for the guy in the book I had started earlier this morning. I had only been reading for the last two hours, hanging onto the edge of the damn sofa to get to this point.

I hadn't been able to eat, sleep, or move until I read about how she finally admitted she loved the sucker.

"Are you going to shower, babe?" Richard asked from the kitchen, sipping on a green protein shake. Scrunching my nose at his choice of a meal, I shook my head.

"Not right now. Need to finish this," I muttered, rereading the last sentence again.

"I don't know why you bother reading those. They all end the same," he continued the conversation, and I sighed, knowing I had to put the book down. Once he started, I wouldn't be able to concentrate.

"What do you mean?" I asked, sticking my bookmark between the pages and closing the book.

"Boy meets girl. She, for some reason, won't be with him, even though she's attracted, and same for the guy. But then, something tragic happens, and they end up together. Then, boom—they fall in love." He finished his protein shake with a burp, and I rolled my eyes.

Typical pig.

"I still don't understand why you're questioning why I read. Every book is different." He shook his head, leaving his glass in the sink for me to rinse and put in the dishwasher. He'd grown up being an only child, and his mother just about kissed the ground he walked on, so he didn't understand the concept of doing chores.

"Seems like a waste of time to me when, you know, they are going to end up together." He headed for our bedroom, shrugging his shoulders.

"What else would you propose I do?" I asked, humoring him while I pick up the book again.

"Me, of course!" He slammed the door behind him just as I considered tossing one of the decorative pillows at his head.

Pig.

Ignoring him, I got lost between the pages again. A few minutes later, he headed out for his pre-game run, leaving me with peace and quiet.

* * *

A FEW HOURS LATER, I had finished my book, cleaned our apartment, loaded the dishwasher, and showered. After looking over my reflection, I gathered my long, black hair into a ponytail, curled the ends, and swiped a layer of pink gloss to my lips.

It was hot outside today, and the jersey I had to wear with Richard's last name on it was thick and heavy, making the already unbearable heat suffocating.

I paired his jersey with a pair of cut-off jean shorts, hoping to at least to catch a tan while watching the game. Sticking my ponytail through the back of a baseball cap for the Atlanta Braves, I slid on my Ray Bans and exited the bathroom.

Scarlett was waiting for me in the lounge, channel surfing while her husband, Matt, scrolled through his phone. She threw the controller to the coffee table and stood. "About damn time. I don't want to have the worst seats, you know?" Matt rolled his eyes but stood and followed her to the front door.

"You do know we have assigned seats, right?" I grabbed my keys and bag from the kitchen and then locked the front door behind us.

"Don't waste your breath, Logan. Scar here thinks it's a lotto system." Scarlett flushed and shoved her boyfriend.

"I do not think that, you oaf. I was just being dramatic because you are late, as usual." She pointed at me as we exited the building and got into Matt's white Wrangler.

"Whatever. Sue me for wanting to look good for Rich. You know he likes to take a picture after the game with the paps to show everyone he's not a playboy."

Matt and Scarlett shared a look but didn't say anything as we merged onto the highway toward the stadium where the Atlanta Braves were expected to play the Tampa Bay Rays in just two hours. Richard hadn't voiced his concerns with me, but I knew he was nervous about the game, mostly because of some player he mentioned his coach was interested in trading.

Said player would be sharing the role of pitcher with Richard, and he hated the idea of an alternative for days when his coach thought he wasn't good enough.

"Do you know anything about the other team?" Scarlett asked, fiddling with the radio station until Luke Combs's voice crooned through the speakers.

"Not much, but Rich is nervous. They must be worthwhile competition then."

"I hear Jaxon Dexter is cute." She swiveled around in her seat to wiggle her brows at me suggestively. "The perfect step in the right direction away from Richard."

"You do know I am sitting right here?" Matt asked his girl-friend, and she scoffed.

"Of course, honey. I'm looking for a man for my best friend because Richard isn't her forever man."

"What happened to not getting involved?" He flipped the turn signal and exited the highway, joining a long line of cars waiting to get into the stadium.

Scarlett huffed, crossed her arms over her chest, and looked out the window. "Seriously, Matthew, I hate when you do that."

And I seriously hated being the one in the middle of their lover spat.

"Do what? Remind you of the things you said you wouldn't do at home not even an hour ago?" He chuckled, but Scarlett wasn't amused in the slightest.

Turning to face me, she ignored her boyfriend, who meant well, and placed her hand on my knee.

"You know I mean well, right? Even though this idiot drives me crazy, I want you to be happy like I am. I don't want you to be miserable anymore." She squeezed my leg. I knew exactly what she was trying to do; it was what she always did. Taking care of people was what she loved to do most. It was probably why she became a nurse.

Blinking back the sudden prickling behind my eyes, I rested my hand on hers and squeezed. "I know, Scar. I know."

"I hate it when you two get all emotional, man," Matt groaned, and Scarlett giggled.

"You're just jealous, honey." She turned back to the front and reached for his hand, their fingers interlocking on the center console.

She wasn't wrong. I wanted what she had with Matt. I wanted that delirious kind of love. The type that knocked me off my feet and showed me exactly what I had been missing in life. The kind of love my parents had.

* * *

WE LOST the first game of the season, and Richard was a sore loser. I watched from the stands as he chucked his glove to the dirt and shouted angrily at his coach.

We'd only been together for a year, and the more I observed his behavior, the more I found to hate about him. Regardless, I waited for him like always with Scarlett and Matt at my side, but today, he didn't reach for me. Instead, he shoved the cameras out of his face and stormed past me and the rest of his fans like I was just some girl he didn't know.

"What the hell was that about?" Scar wrapped her hand around my forearm as the fans shoved past us to get to him and the other teammates.

"Sore loser," I mumbled, watching his team follow behind him, heads bent down in disappointment, their girlfriends and wives at their sides.

"We have dinner at Matt's parents' tonight, but we can drop you off at home." She played with a lock of my hair, soothing my racing heart at Richard's rejection.

"Uh, yea, if you don't mind," I stuttered, looking at the empty spot where he'd walked past me. "I can't believe he did that," I whispered, turning to her. Without my sunglasses covering my eyes, she could see the tears pooling, and her smile faded.

"It'll be okay. Maybe he didn't see you." She pulled me into a hug, and I sniffled, trying my hardest to keep the tears at bay.

"Maybe."

She led me to Matt's Jeep and sat in the backseat with me, wiping away the few stray tears that fell before helping me reapply my lip gloss. She pulled a brush through my knotted hair and squirted some perfume on my neck during the short drive.

"Now, you're going to walk in there and demand answers. I don't care if he lost. You're his girlfriend, and he shouldn't have treated you like that. I'm a phone call away, okay?" I wrapped my arms around her neck and pulled her into a hug.

"You're the best. I don't know what I'd do without you. And Matt, you better take care of her. This one is special, and if you hurt her... Well, I'll just have to kill you." My voice cracked, and Matt chuckled, his eyes focused on Scarlett, so much love shining in them.

"I couldn't hurt her. She'd hurt me first. You know that."

"Damn right and don't you ever forget it," she chirped, getting us all to laugh.

I exited the Wrangler and waved as they pulled away. Entering the lobby of the apartment building, I greeted the doorman, who smiled at me and bowed his head.

"I heard they lost?" He frowned, and I nodded.

"Unfortunately, but they can't always win, I guess." Shrugging, I bid him goodbye and headed down the hall to our shared apartment.

Unlocking the door, I pushed it open and paused at the sight of his discarded shoes. Next to them were a smaller pair of white tennis sneakers, but they weren't mine.

Don't overthink.

He wouldn't cheat.

Take a deep breath.

It's going to be okay.

"Rich, are you home, baby?" My voice shook as I kicked off my sneakers and dropped my bag on the couch.

There wasn't an answer, but our bedroom door was closed. I knew I left it open earlier.

"Richard?" I called again, holding my phone in my shaking hand.

He cursed from behind the door, and then, there was move-

24

ment. Before I could twist open the doorknob, he was throwing it open, bare-chested.

"Hey, babe," he said, running a hand through his messy hair. Running my eyes over him, my eyes tracked the red lipstick marks on his neck and jaw.

"Who's in there?" I whispered, my heart threatening to pound right out of my chest.

"No one. I was just about to shower," he lied, but he wouldn't let me into our bedroom.

"Who's in there, Richard?" I asked again, this time anger lacing my tone, and his eyes hardened.

He let the door open, and there, lying in our bed, was some young girl with red lips. Her hair was ruffled, her eyes big and wild as she watched the encounter. There was no shame in her expression. She waved, her lips tilting into a smile.

"Are you going to join us?" She sounded young, and despite the false bravado she was portraying, I saw fear in her eyes.

"You pig." I stuck my finger in Richard's chest, and he had the audacity to grin. "How dare you?!" I screamed, storming past him to get to my closet.

"What are you doing, babe?" He followed me into the walk-in closet as I shoved a few of my things into a duffle bag. He then followed me into the bathroom, where I swiped all my makeup products into the bag.

"Leaving. We are done, Richard."

"Babe, wait—let me explain." He gripped my elbow, but I yanked my arm out of his hold.

"Don't touch me! I am done with this relationship. I don't want to ever see you again. I'll come by when you are at practice to get the rest of my things, but I am leaving now!" I threw whatever my fingertips touched into the bag, zipped it closed, and rushed out of the room, away from the whore in our bed.

"Good! Leave! I didn't like you that much anyway. And you know what, Logan?" Stopping in the center of our apartment, my chest rising and falling with adrenaline, I looked at him. His hair was messy from her fingers, his cheeks were flushed, and his eyes were wild. And he was naked except for a pair of black boxers.

"What?" His face twisted into a sneer, and I braced myself.

"You were fucking terrible in bed. I would have been better off with a mannequin than you. I had to find someone else to satisfy my needs." Rushing out of the apartment, I slammed the door in his face before he could see the tears streaming down my cheeks.

CHAPTER 4

Jaxon

Four Months Ago

Sitting beside Luke on the bench in the pits, I worked through the breathing routine Coach taught us.

Inhale.

Exhale.

It did little to calm my racing heart or ease my nerves, but my muscles relaxed the slightest bit. I had to catch their eye.

We were playing against the team I wanted to be part of: the Atlanta Braves. They were fierce competition, but I wasn't afraid of losing—not today. We *had* to win.

"You can do this, man. Here's to throwing a record-breaking pitch." Luke clapped me on the back. As he adjusted his hat, I saw the nerves in his eyes. Last year when we played this team, their pitcher, Richard Balmer, had thrown dirty and cost us the whole game, and the referee had sided with their coach.

We were all a little tense and anxious for today, but I was determined to show his coach I was better. He needed me more than him, and my coach understood my need for a change. He had a family at home, too.

"As long as you get us at least three home runs, buddy." He grinned, white teeth bright in the dark pit.

"Yeah, no pressure, right? How many times have you thrown a hundred mile-per-hour pitch?" He scratched his jaw. "Oh, that's right—you haven't." He chuckled, shaking his head. "You've got it in you. I overheard Coach talking to someone on the phone about it. You just don't believe in yourself."

Hundred mile-per-hour pitches were rare but becoming increasingly more common. The Braves' pitcher had yet to throw one, and I was hoping if I could, that would seal my fate.

Rolling my neck, the tight muscles loosened. I twisted my back, and the joints popped. "No time like the present, right?"

The stadium was packed. Our side was a brilliant sea of navy blue, yellow, and white, fans screaming as we exited the dugout. The cleat chasers held signs up, asking us to marry them, our jersey numbers printed on big cardboard signs. Cowbells rang, and adrenaline surged through my veins.

The other side of the stadium, decked out in navy, scarlet, and white, also cheered as their team joined us. We stood in line for the national anthem, my heart beating so loudly, I could barely make out the voice of the young girl standing in the middle of the field, pouring her heart out.

"Let's play ball!" The umpire screamed and the game started. Standing on the mound, I stared down the stretch to the other player. He was waiting for me—the whole arena was.

Inhale.

Exhale.

Inhale.

Raising my knee, I prepared for my first pitch of the game. Tightening my fingers around the ball, I exhaled, and the ball soared from my fingers and straight into the glove of the catcher.

The umpire raised his fist, signaling the first strike. The announcer's voice filled the field, and a collective gasp rang from the Braves' side of the arena.

Preparing myself again, I closed my eyes.

Inhale.

Silence fell across the buzzing stadium.

Exhale.

I lifted my knee and twisted my body.

Inhale.

Exhale.

Pitching the ball toward the batter, I waited. There was a loud crashing sound as the ball connected with the bat, and chaos erupted as the ball went soaring. The Braves' player dropped his bat and ran like his ass was on fire.

He made the first home run of the game, and the crowd burst into cheer. Our side was deadly silent as I prepared for the next batter. The guy grinned at me, jutting out his chin with arrogance, trying to throw me off my game.

Like always, I breathed, honing in on the silence and letting it calm me. Pitching the ball toward the arrogant player, it hit the catcher's glove.

The umpire once again raised his fist. The announcer then informed the crowd of the strike. The batter scowled, tapped the dirt with his bat, and then lowered to his position. I waited for the umpire's signal and then pitched the second ball to my catcher.

Again, the announcer let the crowd know of the second strike.

The player was now getting angry, his body tensing as I prepared for the third pitch. I rolled my shoulders and waited for my signal. Sweat rolled down my neck into the hem of my shirt. The thick material stuck to my back, and I itched to tear it off.

Throwing the third pitch, the bat clapped off the ball, and it soared over our heads. The batter dropped the bat and made it to first base before the Rays had possession of the ball.

When the Braves were close to getting their second home run, the player struck out. The batter from before was hovering on second base, waiting to finish this, but the last two batters also struck out. One more and Luke would have a chance at a home run, and I'd get a chance to rest my arm.

The announcer informed the crowd of what was happening. There was a mix of emotion from both sides as the next batter took the plate again. I pitched the first ball to my catcher.

Everyone was on the edge of their seats as I threw the second, straight to the catcher again. Someone screamed, but I wasn't letting anyone distract me.

"Ladies and gentlemen, did you see that?" The ball was flying above our heads as the Braves' landed another hit before we caught the ball and tagged the batter on the second base. "Pitcher Jaxon Dexter just threw a 105 mile-per-hour pitch!"

Holy fuck. I did it. I beat my own record.

The announcer started to talk about my record, my past, and how I was related to Dante Dexter. I tuned out my stats and turned to find Luke raising his fist to the sky and the rest of my team cheering for me.

I glanced up toward the box where the Braves' team owner was sitting, I couldn't see much through the tinted glass, but I hoped he saw that I was worth the chance.

* * *

WE WON 17 TO 15. It was a close call, but Luke hit the winning home run. Coach shook our hands and nodded at me with silent congratulations for my new record.

After the game, we piled into the guest locker room, taking turns in the four shower stalls, washing the sweat and grime from our bodies. The summer sun had wiped us of all our energy, and the usual locker room ball-busting was minimal today.

"Fix things with Melanie?" I asked Luke as he dressed, while I shoved all my belongings into my duffle.

"Oh, yeah. We're all good now. I need to call her. She was gonna watch the game from home." His smile was big as he pulled me in for a one-armed hug. "You did fucking good today, Dexter. If they don't trade you, it's their loss."

"Time will tell, I guess. Are we goin' out tonight, boys?" Everyone's mutual agreement filled the space, bouncing off the walls, and Luke quickly found a local bar after a quick search on his phone. We settled on a time and then left the safety of the locker room to where the paparazzi, friends and family, and cleat chasers were waiting.

All of them were hungry for a piece of us.

Richard Balmer shoved past me on his way out of the Braves locker room. He'd been known to be a sore loser in the league, so I brushed it off, thinking nothing of the exchange.

Excitement filled the air of the bus back to the hotel, where everyone went their own ways to recover from the afternoon heat before a night of drinking. We had to be at the airport tomorrow morning for a flight back home, where all of us would be nursing hangovers.

Gage's name lit up the screen of my phone. Accepting the call, I held the device to my ear.

"What did you think?" I asked, shutting the door to my hotel room behind me and flipping the lock and deadbolt. I dropped my duffle bag to the ground as he sighed.

"Didn't know you were that good. Shit, that was amazin'. What did it feel like?" His voice was full of excitement and, surprisingly, awe.

"I wanted to show them I was worth a chance. Hopefully, they'll recruit me for the team. I heard they were lookin' for another pitcher." Falling to the bed, I laid there, staring at the ceiling, listening to Gage's deep breaths.

"When will you find out?" There was some commotion in the background. A dog barked, a child cried, and he sighed.

"They should have a decision by the mornin', but usually, I'd know by now." Worry crept into my voice, and from the silence that followed on the other end, I knew he had stepped away from his own problems to help with mine.

"What's the process? Is it like the NFL? They need to ask your coach, right?" He knew I wanted to come back home; I had mentioned it a few months ago, and at the time, he had suggested approaching the Braves' owner, but that was unheard of.

"My coach knows I want to make a switch to be closer to you guys, and he's fine with it. The other coach will have to ask him and then will approach me with an offer."

"And if they don't offer, what's your backup plan?" Gage asked.

"Then, I stay with the Rays for another season and try again. My friend, Luke, mentioned the Marlins are lookin' for a pitcher, but I want to get out of Florida. I'm tired of the humidity and old people." He chuckled.

"You sure you don't just miss us? Didn't seem like you wanted to leave the last time we all got together." He wasn't wrong. Visiting and leaving was getting harder because I was seeing the life I was missing out on.

"Right, as if I'm even thinkin' about settlin' down and gettin' married like you fools. I still have a few wild years left." There was more humor in my tone than seriousness, but I really wasn't ready. The thought of a girl to come home to and kids terrified me.

"One day, she's gonna come into your life and knock you so hard on your ass, you'll be beggin' her to keep you. You'll want it all. The house, kids, even the fuckin' dog, because you'll be happy. But until you meet her, you won't understand what I'm sayin'." His words filled the silence, their weight heavy. He sighed when Carter called for him. "Look, man, I gotta go, but don't give up. You deserve this. You're a natural, and I am so proud of you."

Clearing my throat of the emotion burning there, I swallowed. "Thanks. I have big boots to fill. I only hope I can do that."

"You've already filled them. Stop worryin' about Dad and us.

We wouldn't care if you never played a damn sport again. Just be happy. I'll see you soon, okay?"

"Yeah. I have a week off comin' up. I'll fly up to see y'all."

Ending the call, I let the phone drop to the mattress. Closing my eyes, I breathed in the stale hotel room air.

I beat my own record today.

A moment I wished I could have shared with my dad and all my brothers.

CHAPTER 5

Logan

FOUR MONTHS AGO

Wiping away the tears streaming down my flushed cheeks, I shoved the few belongings I'd grabbed from the apartment into the trunk of my car and sat in the driver's seat, letting the sting of betrayal burn.

I couldn't call Scarlett. She'd leave her soon-to-be in-laws in a flash to come beat Richard up. All five feet of her would storm in there and wreak absolute havoc.

Instead, I cried until my eyes hurt, my throat burnt, and I longed for a bottle of beer. Down the street, the local bar was filling up with people. The parking lot had quickly filled up, and people were waiting in a long line to get in.

Joe's had been my first place of employment, and the owner had been friends of my parents. It seemed like the best idea to nurse a beer with him behind the bar. Anything to distract me.

Pulling the sun visor down, I opened the tiny mirror and fixed my smudged makeup. Reapplying my black eyeliner and mascara, I brushed some pink blush to my cheeks, hoping to hide my blotched skin, and then swiped some pink gloss to my lips.

After moving my car into Joe's parking lot, I made my way

inside just as the sun set, casting the world into darkness. The small, poorly-lit bar was at capacity with rowdy baseball players and fans. The place was covered in people sporting Tampa Bay Rays merchandise, and I cringed at the sight of the players loitering at the bar.

"What brings you by, dear?" Joe's raspy voice caught my attention just as I considered darting out. He was leaning against the corner of the bar, wiping down the counter.

"Just needed to be around someone familiar." I came to stand by his side, noticing that there wasn't a barkeep tonight. "Are you short-staffed tonight?" There was a knowing twinkle in his eye, the same my mom used to get when I used to crawl into her lap as a child after a bad day at school.

"Unfortunately, Mark's wife went into labor earlier, and I didn't realize there was a big game." One of the players raised his hand to get Joe's attention, and I quickly rounded the bar.

"No worries. I'll help out. Nothing's changed since I was in college, I'm assuming?" Joe cracked a weathered grin.

"Haven't changed a thing since your mother helped me arrange this place." My father and Joe had been best friends growing up, and naturally, my mother became the third musketeer to all their shenanigans. When my dad died from a surgery complication, Joe stepped up and took care of me and Mom, and then when my mom died from cancer, he took me under his wing as though I was always his little girl.

"I need the distraction," I told him, heading toward the baseball player, who still had his hand raised.

Like most players, his skin was tan from the sun, his teeth perfectly white, which paired well with a grin that I was sure got a lot of girls to drop their skirts, but not me.

"What can I get ya?" I noted his empty glass and saw the guy to his left skim his dark eyes over me. I looked over his dark features— black hair, perfect tan, and a chiseled jaw. I couldn't help but wonder just how many girls he had gotten with his eyes alone.

"Whatever you have on draft. My girl swears that all women have good taste, so surprise me." His friend cracked a smile and shook his head.

"Melanie is a fool, but so are you." His friend threw his head back and finished the last swig of his Corona. "I'll have another Corona, unless you can recommend something better?" he asked me, and I thought back to my college days, when I thought beer tasted good.

"Couldn't advise you on beer. I drank too much in college, and now, I can't stand it. Corona was good, but only for social drinking. You're celebrating tonight, so you should try the Blue Moon Belgian White in a bottle and the Firestone Walker on draft." Both boys nodded in appreciation.

"So, you've watched the game today, know your beer, and went to college. Aren't you a catch?" The guy who had a girlfriend asked, nudging his friend and wiggling his brows. "Sounds like you should get to know her."

His friend shook his head at his friend. "I don't date. We'll take those beers."

Handing them their drinks a moment later, I nodded at Mr. Tall, Dark, and Mysterious. "I don't date either."

The friend cracked up with laughter and raised his drink to me. "Imagine that—a girl who doesn't want you, man? I love it! What's your name?" He was friendly and kind, and just what I needed tonight.

"Logan, and you guys?"

"I'm Luke, and this buzz kill over here is my friend, Jaxon. Usually, he's better company. You'd think he'd be happy we won today, right?" He nudged Jaxon, who rolled his eyes.

"Jaxon, as in Jaxon Dexter, the guy who pitched that 105 mile-per-hour ball today?" Luke's eyes went big.

"Don't tell me you're a cleat chaser in disguise. You actually were there?"

"Not a cleat chaser. My, uh, ex is one of the Braves." Jaxon perked up. Leaning forward, he rested both his elbows on the counter and stared at me.

"Who's your ex?"

"Doesn't matter. Can I get you two anything else?" He settled back into his seat, arms crossed over his chest.

"We're good for now, sweetheart. Come by in ten minutes with refills. We're celebratin' tonight." Noticing the slight twang in his tone, I noted he wasn't from Florida.

Moving away from the pair, I filled the orders of some of the other players, who were just as kind. Most of them told me briefly about their wives or girlfriends as I refilled their drinks.

"I forgot how good you are with the guests." Joe leaned against the back of the bar as I took a small break. "How about a drink? Looks like you could use one." He was offering me a small shot glass filled to the brim with clear liquid.

Taking the shooter from him, I threw my head back and swallow the tequila. It burned all the way down my throat, warmth settling in my stomach. Some of the guys near me cheered at my execution, but I gave them my back. I wasn't here to impress them.

"How'd you know?"

"Overheard your conversation with those two over there," he said, jerking his head the tiniest bit in Luke and Jaxon's direction. "When did things end with you and Richard?" He nursed a beer, his eyes roaming the room before settling back on me.

"When I walked into our apartment and found him cheating on me." He poured me another shot, and just as I was about to throw my head back, Luke called out to me.

"Hey, Logan, get us two of those!" Joe handed me two more shot glasses, and I poured the drinks before putting them in front of Luke, who was grinning. "Now, go get yours. It's not fun to do shots alone." Joe was already in front of me, handing me the shot before I could reject.

"On three," Jaxon said, his deep voice sending a shock wave down my spine. "One, two—"

"Three," I said, throwing my head back and downing the liquid, welcoming the warmth.

An hour later and four more shots down, I was no longer helping Joe man the bar. Instead, I was barely sitting upright on my barstool next to Luke, who was slurring his words with every story he told me.

I knew all about how Luke and Jaxon became friends. I knew that Jaxon had three brothers and was from a small town in the middle of nowhere. I'd heard all about Melanie, Luke's girlfriend, who he wanted to marry, and I also knew that Jaxon Dexter did not talk a lot.

"I think it's time you went back to the hotel, man," Jaxon interrupted Luke when he started to tell me how he thought Jaxon was a class-A douche bag for the third time. "She's already heard that story."

Luke flushed and then looked down at his phone. "Yeah, alright. Mel should still be up—might even be in the mood for some fun," he wiggled his brows, "if you know what I mean." He stood and staggered out the bar, some of his teammates following.

"Aren't..." I looked after them and tried to form a coherent thought that would hopefully turn into a sentence. "Aren't you worried?" My words were slurred, and my tongue was heavy. The music was too loud, and I just wanted to close my eyes and sleep right there on the bar.

"Nah. He'll make it to the hotel. You, on the other hand—you don't look good." He pushed a glass of lemon water in front of me, the same one he'd ordered for himself ten minutes ago.

"I'm not much of a drinker," I said, sipping on the cold liquid.

"You could have fooled me, sweetheart." He pushed a hand through his thick hair, and I longed to feel the strands between my fingers.

"My college days are over." He chuckled at my response as I held my head up on the bar with one hand.

"You barely look a day over twenty-one."

"Flattery won't get you into my pants, Dexter." He snorted, looking around the bar that was getting quieter as the early morning hours rolled around.

"Not interested in sex, sweetheart. It only gets people into trouble. You remind me of my sisters-in-law."

"And how is that?"

"Like the world keeps eatin' you up and spittin' you out without givin' you a chance to recover." Joe convinced the last few people to leave, and then it was just Jaxon and I at the bar, staring each other down.

"Alright, Logan. How are you getting home, dear?" Joe asked, wiping down the bar one last time.

"I'll take her." Joe's eyes lifted to Jaxon and then to me, waiting my consent. I nodded, too tired and drunk to care. I didn't have a home right now.

I hadn't thought that far ahead.

My car was the only thing I had—the only safe place to go.

Standing from the bar stool, I swayed on the heels I had stuffed my feet into before walking into the bar.

Jaxon's big, warm hand rested on my back, and then, his arm wrapped around my torso, pulling me into his side, steadying me.

Outside, a soft breeze blew across my heated cheeks. "How come you aren't toasted?" I ask, hiccupping.

"I stopped drinkin' an hour ago and switched to water while you and Luke kept on with the shots. Tequila is never a friend. Surprised you didn't learn that in college."

"Maybe I wanted to forget tonight," I mumbled, seeing my white Kia Soul in the parking lot. It was the only car left. Heading toward it, Jaxon's grip around my waist tightened.

"Where are you goin'?"

"Home?" I questioned, pointing to the car.

"You do know you are well above the legal limit," he sighed, and I nodded.

"That's my home tonight," I slurred, and understanding flashed in his eyes.

"He broke up with you after the game, didn't he?" I didn't want to answer. I wasn't ready to deal with the pity or the reality of what happened only a few hours ago.

"Can you make me forget?" I turned into his chest, my fingers curling into the black fabric of his t-shirt. His big hands wrapped around my forearms, setting my skin on fire.

"The tequila should help with that," he whispered, leaning his head toward mine, his nose brushing my temple.

The intoxicating scent of his cologne was driving me wild, and all I wanted in that moment was to feel his lips against mine, to slide my fingers into his thick, dark hair. To forget.

"Please make me forget him?"

He brushed his nose to mine, and I held my breath.

"Are you sure, sweetheart? I leave in the mornin'." His lips whispered against my heated cheek, and I nearly melted into a puddle right at his feet.

"Don't make me ask again, Jaxon. I won't beg." Sliding his hands down my forearms, he unclenched my fists from his shirt and slid the fingers of his one hand into mine. He fit perfectly...like he was made to find me.

"My hotel's this way." His voice was like silk against my skin, the twang in his drawl igniting a fire in my veins.

I needed him.

I needed him *everywhere*.

CHAPTER 6

Jaxon

Sunlight streamed into my bedroom of the penthouse I'd fallen in love with a week ago after signing with the Atlanta Braves. Their current pitcher, Richard Balmer, was on his way out, and I was going to be the lucky one to fill his position.

For the next season, I'd play as his backup, but the Braves' coach and team owner had taken a liking to me. And surprisingly, they knew my brothers, which helped sway their choice of offering me a chance.

It wasn't my 105 mile-per-hour pitch, although that had gained me quite the following, and because of it everyone had higher expectations of me. It was my family history, one brother in the NFL and two that tried, our name was popular in the sports industry.

My alarm went off again, and I reached for my phone on the bedside table to silence it. Peace filled the room once again.

Just as I was about to fall back asleep, exhausted from yesterday's training, the phone buzzed in my hand. Answering the call without checking the caller ID, I immediately regretted it.

"You better be out of bed, man." Luke was a morning person —always had been—and I had always been a night owl. Sometimes, I wondered how we got along.

"You damn well know I'm still in bed. I told you how late practice ran last night," I grumbled, sliding a hand down my face and rubbing my tired eyes.

"I also know that you have your first game in a week, and you want to be pitching rather than keeping the bench warm, right?" Sometimes, I hated the fucker.

Times like right now because he was right.

Richard was the only player on the team who took an immediate dislike to me, not that it was any surprise, but he was making it hard to be accepted by spreading rumors.

He'd already told everyone I took steroids the day I threw my record-breaking pitch, and some believed him.

"That dipshit start anything new?" Luke asked and I sighed.

"Half the guys keep checking to make sure I'm not taking steroids, the others could care less, but Coach is breathing down my neck." Sitting up, I stood from the bed and stumbled into my bathroom.

"What about that bartender, Logan? Bump into her yet?" Since Luke had proposed to Melanie and picked a date for their upcoming wedding, he was hell-bent on finding me a date. He reminded me a few times a week it was time to start looking for a girl to take home and settle down with.

"I'm not goin' near her, man. Remember, her ex is one of my teammates. That's a can of worms I don't want to open anytime soon." He chuckled.

"When has that ever stopped you? You're Jaxon Dexter. Whatever you want, you take."

Logan had been a mistake.

A mistake I didn't want to make twice.

I had fallen for her green eyes, and the moment she opened

those pretty pink lips and mentioned one of my favorite beers, I was a goner.

Most women didn't know a thing about beer, but she was well-versed, and after watching her throw her slender neck back for a shot, I wanted her in my bed.

"It was a mistake—" I started to tell him, but he erupted into laughter.

"Bullshit. Don't lie to me. She was still in your bed the next morning we left. You never let them stay," he reminded me. He'd made fun of me the entire flight home and told Melanie all about the bartender who'd changed me.

"She had nowhere to go," I argued, thinking back to the conversation I shared with her in the early hours of the morning.

I was pretty sure the alcohol made her spill all her secrets about her ex, but she still withheld a name and refused to go into detail. All I knew was that they dated for a while, and he was terrible in bed. She'd thanked me for making her see stars and for being gentle.

Hell, I'd never been complimented in bed before. He must have been useless.

She humbled me in one night, and when I woke the next morning, her soft, black hair tickling my nose as she cuddled into my chest, I was sure I had died and gone to Heaven.

Never in all my years did I ever think a woman could make me want more than one night.

But Logan did.

She showed me in one night what I could have.

"You daydreaming about her, man? No time for that now. We have a run to go on." Groaning, I brushed my teeth and changed into a pair of joggers. We'd been running together over the phone to motivate each other, and sometimes I hated it.

"Has anyone ever told you that you're fuckin' annoyin'?" He chuckled as I laced up my sneakers.

"All the damn time, man. Have you met Mel? I think she tells me ten times a day."

"And somehow, she's still marryin' your sorry ass."

* * *

Checking my reflection, I adjusted my tie one last time before stepping into the room where my coach was sitting at a table with the team owner and a reporter.

It was time to announce my arrival to the Atlanta Braves. I hadn't told my family the news about me getting signed yet.

After today, I wouldn't be able to hide it anymore. My arrival to this team was breaking news in the league, especially with Richard Balmer's retirement coming soon.

"You'll just answer a few questions, but your coach will do most of the talkin', okay, hun?" the older reporter told me, reading over her notepad. I nodded, my tongue dry from nerves. "Congrats on the team swap, by the way. The Braves are my favorite." She winked and then prepped Coach with the questions she was going to ask him.

I took my seat, adjusting my suit jacket, wishing I could just rip it off and undo the tie wrapped around my neck.

An Atlanta Braves team hat was laying on the table, and the agent handed it to me. I put the stiff hat on my head and stared ahead at the camera.

"Going live in three, two, one," the cameraman said, and the reporter stood in front of him, a fake smile tugging at her bright red lips.

"Good evening, Atlanta! Behind me is the Atlanta Braves' hottest new player. He started his career late in the game, but he's been taking the league by storm. You know his brother, Dante Dexter, but have you met Jaxon Dexter?" The cameraman turned the big device to me, and sweat rolled down my neck.

I waved, unsure what was expected but kept a grin plastered to my face. *I want to be here.* As nerve-wracking as this was, I wanted to be here on this team.

"You caught the coach's eye at a game last season, is that right?" she asked, and I paused.

What was I supposed to say?

"I hope so. I played for the Tampa Bay Rays last season, and when we played against the Braves', I threw my first ever three-digit mile-per-hour pitch." She nodded, and from the corner of my eye, I saw Coach did, too.

"What did that feel like, Jaxon? You're late to the sport, so you must have put in a lot of extra work to get to this point."

"Funny enough, I didn't know I had hit 105 until the announcer screamed it. I think I was in shock. It felt like every other time I had thrown the ball, except I put everythin' I had into that throw." She grinned, and it eased my nerves. Talking about baseball had become therapy.

"So, tell us why you chose baseball and not football like your brothers."

This was the question I wasn't sure how to answer. It was fun to play with my brothers and dad, but without them, I hated it.

"I grew up playin' football. I think as soon as I could run, my dad had me out in our backyard, playin' with my brothers. He wanted all of us to play pro, but only Dante made it. I was following his path until I realized I wasn't enjoyin' the sport anymore. We all played baseball during the off-season to stay in shape, and it just made sense. Plus, I don't have to run as much." I winked, earning laughter from everyone in the room.

"When can we expect to see you on the field?" she asked, and I turned to Coach because ultimately, it was his decision.

"Hopefully soon. I'm still learnin' the dynamics of the team, and I don't want to step on anyone's toes, you know?" She nodded as if I had just given her the perfect segway to start talking about Balmer.

She turned her attention to Coach, and the tension eased from my body, the bright lights no longer on me.

She questioned Coach and the team owner and then ended her segment. I was relieved it was over, but from the buzzing coming from my pocket, the buzzing that hadn't stopped for the last ten minutes, my family now knew. Which meant I had to deal with the consequences of not telling them first.

Coach shook my hand and then the team owner. I thanked them for what felt like the hundredth time and then exited the building, the fall breeze cooling me down.

Pulling my phone from my pants pocket, I cringed at the caller ID.

"Hey, Ma," I answered, getting into my black F-150.

"Hey, Ma? Is that all you've got to say, young man?" She paused. I could hear dad in the background and waited. "Why didn't you tell us you were goin' to the Braves? And why haven't you come to visit if you're so close?!" She wasn't asking, that was for damn sure.

"I wanted to surprise you, that's all. Is everyone there?" I sighed, gripping the steering wheel.

"Oh, we're all here, brother," Dante said, chuckling. "You could have made me sound better, you know. That reporter loved me." His wife, Brooklyn, started to question him about the reporter, and I fought a grin.

I missed them.

I missed the craziness.

"Son, are you happy?" Dad's voice was gruff, tired, weathered, and not what I was expecting.

"I love the game, Dad," I told him, waiting for his approval. Needing it.

"What dad isn't asking, but I will, is where are our season tickets? You better hook us up, little brother," Gage said. Dante wasn't kidding about everyone being there.

"I'll work somethin' out with my coach. But I won't be playin' for the first few games until they announce Balmer's retirement."

"We want to be there when you pitch. I want to see that 105 mile-per-hour pitch in person," Archer said, and somehow, his silent approval of switching to the Braves lifted a weight off my shoulders.

"I'll make sure you all have tickets and merch to wear." I ended the call a few minutes later after promising a trip home with Mom demanding it be soon.

CHAPTER 7
Logan

I'd never been opposed to becoming a mother. I loved kids, so much so that I became an elementary school teacher.

But I wanted everything checked off my list first. I worked with lists; they helped me organize my life and accomplish my goals.

Find love.

Get married.

Buy a house, preferably on the water, with lots of land for all the kids and dogs I want.

Rescue a dog.

Fall pregnant with the man of my dreams.

Raise a beautiful family.

That had been my list, and so far, I'd achieved none of it, and there was now a baby growing inside of me. At first, I thought I was going to find love in Richard, but I'd been digging for too long and came up empty-handed and more disappointed than anything else.

He'd never laid a hand on me, not like the struggles Scarlett had when we were in high school. Most times, he was too weak to kill a bug. But on the flip side, he'd hurt me in many other ways.

I was never good enough.

I didn't look like the other girls, the blondes he seemed to chase after with boobs the size of my head. I worked during the day, which meant early mornings, and he hated being woken when he didn't have practice.

Not to mention, we hadn't had sex since New Year's Eve. He often claimed I was the problem. When, in reality, he wasn't good enough for me.

And because I wasted my time with him, hoping to find my soulmate in a man that was so far from perfect, I was now far from my ten-year plan.

The afternoon bell rang, signaling the end of recess, and my class of fifteen five-year-olds came bounding in, cheeks flushed, hair matted, and eyes wide with excitement. My assistant teacher, Stella, came in after them, her skin glowing from the afternoon sun.

"Alright, everyone. Grab some water and take a seat." I stood, getting their attention. They all slowed to a walk and found their desks.

I'm going to miss this.

Stella turned the lights off, and the kids put their heads to their desks for a quiet moment as I talked about our next project. I got a few excited giggles when I mentioned the stuffed dog they would be taking home and introducing to their families.

I explained the rules—why they had to take pictures with the stuffed dog and how each person would then make a presentation. The most creative student would win based on the class vote.

Stella flipped the lights back on, and they all looked at me expectantly. I showed them a few examples from last year and then showed them Fluffy, the stuffed dog.

We had an hour left of the day, and Stella announced story time, leading the kids to the bright-blue circle mat, where they rushed to find a colored square to sit on.

While she was reading to them, I worked on my email of resignation to the principal. Scarlett suggested a few days ago that I go and find Jaxon and give him the choice of raising this child with me.

I'd laughed at her, but after doing some thinking, I realized it wasn't the worst idea.

Not all men were pigs.

My dad hadn't been, so there was hope for Jaxon. From the little I could remember about that night, he had been kind.

Kind men wanted to raise kids, right?

"Miss Shaw, when do we find out who takes Fluffy home first?" Brett, one of my star students, stood at the edge of my desk, pushing his black glasses up his nose. His blue eyes were big as they peered up at me through the magnifying glass.

"Well, Miss Stella will put all your names in the hat over there," I point toward the fake magician's hat I had, "and we'll pull one out tomorrow." He nodded, buzzing with excitement.

This was the part I was going to miss. This was my favorite age —when they started to spell and read, when they were the most impressionable.

"I can't wait to tell my mommy all about it," he said, walking away.

I got them all lined up at their cubbies. They slung their small backpacks on and were quietly murmuring to each other about the project. When the bell rang, they ran outside to join the car line, and I followed.

For the next hour, I helped them get into their cars and then walked the stragglers to aftercare before returning to my classroom, where I finished off my email, requesting a meeting to speak about my resignation.

At Scarlett's place, she was curled up on the couch, watching some romcom, her laughter infectious as I walked in. Matt was thankfully at work, giving us some alone time.

"Hey, how were the brats?" She paused the movie as I sat beside her on the sofa.

Shaking my head, I sighed at her dislike for kids. She had never been interested in having her own. "They aren't brats, Scar, and they were great. I'm going to miss them and teaching and just my whole life." An unexpected sob burst from my chest.

"Jeez, those pamphlets weren't kidding! You are sensitive." She fished a tissue out of her bra and handed it to me.

"And you're a bitch. I didn't need to read anything to know that," I cried, blowing my nose into the tissue.

"Ouch, but I won't take it to heart. Who said you have to quit your job and change your whole life? All I suggested was letting Mr. Sexy Ass know about his child growing in there." She patted my small bump.

"And what if he wants me to be a full-time mother? What if I want to be a full-time mom? What if he tells me to leave? Then, I'll have to work. Shit, I didn't think, and I already emailed my resignation!" I cried. Bringing my knees up to my chest, I wrapped my arms around them.

"Hun, you need to calm down, or you'll have an anxiety attack, which won't be good for your baby. Stop worrying. Remember how your mom said we were on a path?" I hated when she brought up my mom because every damn time, she was right.

I nodded, not wanting to look up at her.

"She swore we were all on a path, one chosen for us. And everything that happened along our path was part of our journey, and it was meant to happen. That sexy man was put in your path for a reason, Logan, and so is that baby. Now, stop crying, grab some of the pizza I've got in the kitchen, and come watch a movie with me. Soon, we won't be able to do this, and I'm going to miss my best friend." Lifting my head up to look at her, I saw emotion swirling around her eyes.

"Why won't we be able to do this?"

"Because you, my beautiful friend, are going to fall hopelessly in love with that man, and he is going to sweep you off your feet the way you were always meant to be. He's going to take you away from here, away from me, but that's okay."

Following her instructions, I grabbed a slice of the greasy, cheese pizza and snuggled up with her on the couch, mulling over her words.

Falling in love with a hotshot baseball player? Unlikely. Impossible? No.

* * *

WHEN THE WEEKEND finally rolled around, I spent my entire Saturday morning researching Jaxon Dexter, and from a quick Google search, I found out a lot about his older brothers but little about him.

Finally, after paying some online site to do a background check for twenty dollars, I found his address, and surprisingly, he wasn't far from me. He was just an hour away, living in the city near the Atlanta Braves' arena.

Dressing in a loose shirt and leggings, I pulled my long hair back into a ponytail and applied some makeup before leaving Scarlett's apartment with his address in my GPS.

Walking into the posh apartment building, I passed by the lobby security and entered the glass elevator. Pressing the button for the top floor, I prayed the website had been right, and he was living up in the penthouse.

As I ascended the tall building, I rehearsed for the hundredth time what I was going to say to him if he opened the door.

"Hi, remember me, the girl you slept with four months ago? We met in a bar." No. I shook my head at my reflection and cringed.

This is going to be a disaster.

The elevator dinged, and the doors flew open. Slowly stepping out, I admired the decorations and stared at the single door at the end of the short hall.

Pacing the small space, I tried to come up with something better to say. Resting my hands on my belly, I came up blank.

"What would you say, little one?"

No answer, not that I really expected one.

Taking a deep breath, I used all the confidence I had and marched up to the door, raised my fist, and knocked loudly. Here went nothing.

The door swung open, and Jaxon Dexter stood there, shirtless, wearing the gray sweatpants every woman fantasized about, the phone to his ear.

I was frozen, my hand still raised to knock on the door, jaw slack as I ran my eyes over him again.

I didn't remember his eyes being so dark, yet having tiny flecks of green in them. There was a light dusting of hair on his chest, and his physique was still the lean one I remembered from that night. All I remembered was having the time of my life and wanting to repeat it for the rest of my life.

"Luke, I'm goin' to need to call you back." He hung up without letting Luke answer and dropped his hands to his sides.

I opened my mouth and closed it twice before remembering I had to speak.

"Remember me?" I finally said and waved before dropping my hand and closing my eyes. "Of course, you don't. I mean, why would you? You're Jaxon freaking Dexter, and I'm just me," I rambled, completely and utterly embarrassed, yet unable to stop opening my mouth.

"I remember you, Logan. It's impossible to forget someone as beautiful as you." Flushing, I looked at him. He held the door open a little more. "Are you goin' to come in, sweetheart?"

He remembers me.

CHAPTER 8

Jaxon

WHAT THE HELL WAS SHE DOING ON MY DOORSTEP? How had she found me? How did she get past security downstairs?

Why was she even prettier in the light?

How had I missed the freckles across her cheekbones?

I was expecting my pizza delivery, not her when I heard the knock. I'd hung up on Luke because if he heard she was here, I'd never hear the end of it. From the phone buzzing in my hand, he wanted to know what, or rather who, had abruptly ended our call.

Her pretty pink lips opened and closed, her green eyes electric as they scanned over my shirtless chest not once but twice.

Her fist was raised where she had only a moment ago knocked on the door—almost like she was going to knock again.

"Remember me?" She cleared her throat, a rasp to her voice I didn't remember from that night. She waved and then looked at her hand, her eyes bugging out before she dropped it and closed her eyes, taking a deep breath.

Taking in her features, I noted the panic—from her balled fists, to her stiff posture. She opened her eyes that were noticeably puffy and red-rimmed, her face flushed like she'd been crying. *Was it her ex?*

I shouldn't be thinking about it, the desire to protect her, to make the sadness disappear. It wasn't my job. She wasn't mine to worry about.

She was just a one-night-stand that I couldn't shake from my head. A mistake I couldn't make again.

"Of course, you don't. I mean, why would you? You're Jaxon freaking Dexter, and I'm just me." She was rambling, her voice shaking with each word, and it was fucking adorable. She was all bent out of shape over me.

I wasn't sure how anyone could forget her. Not with that raven hair, dark as night, and eyes so big and beautiful, she could have any man on their knees with just one look. Staring at her, the desire to bring her into my bedroom surfaced, consequences be damned.

I could let this continue. I would have a few months ago if a one-night-stand showed up at my door. But she was different.

I didn't want to watch her make a damn fool of herself with all her rambling, as much as I loved hearing her sweet voice. Her eyes were wild with panic and embarrassment.

I wanted to ease her fears. I wanted to be more than a douchebag.

I was tired of breaking hearts. And I really didn't want to break hers.

"I remember you, Logan. It's impossible to forget someone as beautiful as you." Her cheeks were rosy when she snapped her mouth shut and swallowed. I held the door open a little wider, silently inviting her in. When she didn't move, I couldn't fight the grin tugging at my lips any longer.

She's fucking gorgeous.

"Are you goin' to come in, sweetheart?" Her eyes darted between my bare chest, the door, and the floor. There was a flash of hesitancy before she nodded and walked between me and the door frame.

The rich, intoxicating, vanilla scent of her perfume overwhelmed my senses and clouded my judgment as it tickled my nose and filled the air of my apartment. *This was a bad idea.*

Closing the door behind her, I watched her, waiting to see what she did. Her eyes roamed around the room briefly, but nothing held her attention. She glanced at the door that led to my bedroom, and I wondered if she was thinking the same thing as me.

Is she here for more?
Why is she here?
How did she find me?

Just as I was about to ask her intentions, the bell rang, and this time, it was my pizza. The delivery guy handed me the hot box, thanked me for the tip, and left, not a flash of recognition in his gaze.

That was becoming rare these days, and I missed it.

The downside to becoming a famous athlete was the fame that was attached to it. Everyone knew who I was and wanted a piece of me that I wasn't willing to part with.

"You must think I'm a stalker," she started, her fingers fiddling with the hem of her shirt—the one I'd been standing here wondering how to get off. "Well, I guess I am. I mean, I found you, right?" She was rambling again.

"I have to admit I'm pretty damn curious, sweetheart." Placing the hot cardboard box of pizza on the counter, I flipped open the lid. "Hungry?" I looked away from the cheese pizza to see her tongue dart out and lick her lips.

Grabbing two plates from the cabinet, I put two slices on one for her and four for me. Quietly handing her the plate without her confirmation, she smiled, the hint of a dimple appearing in the corner of her mouth.

"Did you hear my stomach?" She blushed, eyes downcast.

"Could hear it outside the door." She giggled at my lame joke, and damn, if I didn't like that. I wanted her to laugh at all my jokes.

"Right, of course, you could. How silly of me." We took a seat at my kitchen counter, where the invitation to my brother's wedding was sitting.

The invitation I had opened before calling Luke for a Hail Mary. I needed a date.

She glanced at the invitation, her eyes skimming the lines, and then, she smiled. "Your brother?"

I nodded, mouth full of the greasy pizza. Emotion swam in her eyes. She swallowed and then took a small bite from her food.

"You don't like weddin's?" I asked, hopping off the barstool to grab a beer from the fridge. "Want one?" She shook her head quickly, so I offered her the only can of soda I had in the fridge, and she nodded.

"Haven't been to many, honestly. I was hoping I'd be married by now."

"Me neither. Just my two brothers'. Why aren't you married?" Sliding the can to her, she snapped it open and took a long sip.

"Starting to think there isn't someone out there for me. What's your excuse for the single life?"

"Been too focused on my career. There hasn't been time for a girl, too. Y'all are high maintenance." She scoffed.

"That's insulting. Some of us aren't high maintenance."

Grabbing another piece from the box, I offered her the last one remaining, but she shook her head.

"Tell me, sweetheart, would you expect Friday night dates?"

"I wouldn't expect them, but I would like them." She held my stare, her eyes sparkling in the bright, kitchen light.

"Alright, so you are the *only* exception." I raised my hands defensively before grabbing both our plates. I stuck them in the dishwasher and turned to her. "So, how about you tell me the real reason you showed up on my doorstep tonight?"

She swallowed, looked at the counter, inspected the marble, and said nothing.

"Would you believe me if I said I was a crazy fan?" She cracked a weak smile, her hands shaking. She quickly hid them under the counter, so I slowly shook my head.

"I wish that was the case. If it were, I wouldn't have just shared my pizza with you."

"What if I wanted to repeat our night from a few months ago?" She was stalling, so I humored her.

"Then, we'd already be in my bed, sweetheart." She blushed, something I'd noticed she did a lot of around me. *I make her nervous.*

"You're telling me girls actually come by here for that?" Disgust flashed across her face but quickly disappeared.

"The girls don't usually get past my security downstairs. So, I'm wonderin' how you did. But that's somethin' we can talk about later." Logan looked away, finding some artwork on my wall pretty damn interesting, her dark hair hiding her expression from me.

There was something different about her. The way her eyes nervously flitted around my place, the smile that seemed perfected, and her eyes that held too much pain for someone so young.

"Logan, is it your ex? Are you in trouble?" I planted both hands on the cold marble and noticed her visibly stiffen, so I relaxed my stance, choosing to lean back on the closed dishwasher and cross my arms over my chest.

"No, he's gone. Hasn't reached out to me in a long time, thank God. I wish I hadn't wasted so much of my time with him." She looked at me again, and I saw the pain clear as day in her green eyes as they shone with just barely-contained emotion.

Whatever the reason was that she found me, she wasn't ready to tell me. And I didn't care. Her presence in the big apartment was welcomed compared to the loneliness I had been struggling with.

Without Luke ten minutes away, I spent a lot of time alone, compared to Florida, where Luke and I spent countless nights in front of my TV playing video games.

My goal of being closer to home hadn't made sense yet because I had been too goddamn scared to go home and face my father after officially quitting football. Whenever I did go home, I avoided Dad at all costs. But now that they knew, things would get better. They had to.

"So, you know what I do for a livin'. What about you?" I changed the subject, hoping to ease the tension from her body, but it only got worse when her nose scrunched and she burst into tears.

What did I say?

"I'm a—" she cried, tears streaking down her rosy cheeks faster than I could round the counter. I gently placed my hands on her arms, not sure if I should be hugging her or running for the hills. *Maybe she's crazy.*

She pressed her face to my chest, her tears hot against my skin. And I knew right then, she wasn't crazy. She was lost just like me.

"A teacher. I was a teacher," she cried, and I couldn't help but thread my fingers through her silky, soft hair.

"What happened, sweetheart?" When she pulled away and looked up at me, her eyes the color of the prettiest emerald I'd ever seen, the breath was sucked straight from my lungs.

"I quit." She wiped her eyes and jumped from the barstool, taking a step away from me. "I'm sorry. I shouldn't have let my emotions get the best of me. God, I must look like such a fool. It's just been a couple of hard months, and I..." she paused, running her hands frantically through her hair, "I need to walk. I need air."

I nodded, sensing the urgency in her movements. I quickly led her to the front door.

"Let's go. I know a place."

She followed me silently, and as we exited my building, we saw the first glimpse of the setting sun. I had chosen the building on the outskirts of the city, purely because I hated the city life. I was a country boy through and through. I loved land and animals—everything the city was not.

We walked around to the back of my building, where we

crossed the road to a small park. It was the reason I picked this building. I loved walking.

There weren't many people on the trail at this time of the day, and as the sky got darker, I wondered what was running through Logan's mind.

I wanted to know more about her.

"I'm sorry for freaking out. You must really think I'm crazy now, huh?" She had stopped at the only water fountain in the park and was bending over for a long drink. When she faced me again, I watched a single droplet of water fall from her pink lips and roll down her chin.

Without thinking, I brushed it away, my thumb making contact with her soft skin. Her hot breath brushed against my hand as she sighed. And just like that, I was stuck back in that moment.

Back on the night we kissed.

And in this moment, I wanted to taste her again. I needed her.

I wanted to be reminded of how good she tasted. I needed to hear her moan my name.

CHAPTER 9
Logan

I REALLY LIKED LISTS.

They helped keep my anxiety under control. Mom was the one who taught me to write everything down when I was overwhelmed and everything was spiraling out of my control.

"*A list you can control. Once you've done the task, you can check it off and move to the next one,*" she had told me, and I held onto that advice.

I made lists in high school of my homework every night. I made a list of all the colleges I wanted to apply to. I made a list of where I wanted to work.

But most importantly, I made a list of how I wanted my life to go. I *needed* to have some control after Mom died.

Find love.

Get married.

Buy a house, preferably on the water, with lots of land for all the kids and dogs I want.

Rescue a dog.

Fall pregnant with the man of my dreams.

Raise a beautiful family.

The list was on a crumpled piece of paper in my wallet, the first one I hadn't been able to achieve, and it burned every time I thought about it.

I made a list for tonight, and as I reached for it in my jeans pocket, I wondered what Jaxon would think. We'd been silently walking this trail for the last thirty minutes while I tried and failed to get my thoughts in order.

Pulling out the piece of paper Scarlett helped me write, I squinted through the darkness at the bright red letters.

Get in car. Check.

Get past lobby security if there is any. Check.

Knock on his door. Check.

Tell Jaxon about our baby.

Instead of telling him the real reason I'd found him, I chickened out, ate his pizza, flirted like my life depended on it, and then nearly had an anxiety attack in his kitchen. *Way to fucking go, Logan.*

Jaxon easily kept my pace as my mind ran rampant with intrusive thoughts that I wished more than anything would shut the hell up.

I wished again for the hundredth time since I found out about this baby that my mom was here. She would know what to do; she always did. Wasn't that the job of a mom? Would I be like her? Would I just know what to do with this baby?

Panic clawed at my throat, and I fought with every breath I had to not let the sob bubble out, but it was no use. My knees buckled, and I hit the dirt, my body failing me.

Jaxon was there, crouching in front of me, his eyes wide and alert with worry for me. A complete stranger that was pregnant with his child. God, if he knew, he'd run. Surely, he'd run far away.

"Logan, it's goin' to be okay, sweetheart." His warm hand latched onto my wrist, rubbing a soft circle into my boiling skin. "I don't know what's wrong, but it will be okay."

I had to tell him.

He was so kind.

I couldn't keep crying and distracting him with silly things.

I had to stop flirting.

He didn't ask any questions. He stayed at my side, surveilling the surrounding area every few minutes, his body hyperaware as I cried like a pathetic child.

I couldn't make the tears stop, and the uselessness I felt made them fall faster. I hated having no control.

It triggered old memories, moments in my life when I hit rock bottom and had to pull myself out of the darkness alone.

If I could do it when my dad died, and again when mom was taken from me by cancer, surely, I could pull my shit together now.

"I'm sorry," I whispered, wiping the tears from my cheeks, hoping some of my makeup remained intact. I wasn't ready for him to see me without it. I wasn't ready to lose another piece of my armor.

"It's okay. Sometimes, life just kicks us down." He was so fucking sweet, it made my heart ache. "Are you ready to walk back to my place?"

I nodded, and he helped me stand. We walked back down the trail in silence. The only sound was the loud chirp of crickets and frogs surrounding us. It gave me time to rein in my emotions, to take back control.

At the door of his lobby, he paused, eyes flickering between me and the door. "You don't want me to come back up?" I could see the hesitation in his dark eyes, from his furrowed brows to his frown.

"It's not that. I just want to know what your expectations are. If you want to go back up there and repeat the other night, I can't. I'm not that guy." He crossed his arms over his chest, muscles rippling with the movement.

He was that guy a few months ago. I had the proof growing in my stomach right now, but I heard the sincerity in his tone, so I kept my lips shut.

"But if you came here for another reason," he hesitated,

grimacing, "to try and be the girl to tame me or some shit, I'm not that guy either. I'm not ready for a relationship. I'm not ready to settle down. I want to focus on baseball. I want to give my all to this season. I can't do that if I have a girlfriend."

I am officially screwed.

He doesn't want me. He doesn't want our baby. I'm alone. I'm going to be a single parent. I can't do this alone. I can't be a mother. I'm not ready. I don't want this.

My mind is exploding with intrusive thoughts as we stand there at the door of his lobby, the bright, white lights shining down on us.

What should I do? How was I supposed to salvage this? What would my mom do? What would Scarlett do?

"I wanted a friend," I stuttered and wanted to shoot myself for saying something so pathetically foolish.

"I don't follow." His posture relaxed. He was no longer on high alert, trying to ward off someone trying to look for a relationship.

"I just got out of a bad relationship. What makes you think I want to dive into another—and with you?" He took a step back, not expecting my comment. Hell, neither was I.

"What's wrong with me?" He jabbed a finger into his chest, all of a sudden defensive.

"Nothing, but I'm not interested in any more baseball players." He chuckled, shaking his head.

"Why me, then, sweetheart? I'm sure you've got some friends."

Why him, Logan? What did you just get yourself into? Tell him the truth.

"Because you need me." A cocky grin took over his beautiful lips, and I fought every bit of desire that rose inside of me.

"And why do I need you?"

Think, Logan! Why does he, the new pitcher of the Atlanta Braves, need you?

"Because my ex is Richard Balmer, and I hear you want to

replace him on the Braves, and I want revenge." I mentally high-fived myself.

"So, he's the asshole who hurt you, huh? Makes sense. He's a lowlife. Funny that you slept with me that night. Seems like fate wanted us to meet, sweetheart."

If only he knew what fate had in store for us. It wanted more than for us to meet. It wanted us to raise a child.

"Do you want to be friends or not?" I didn't have the patience to play this game anymore. I was exhausted, bone tired from crying, and high-strung from anxiety.

"What exactly is your plan?" I didn't have one, but from the gleam in his eye, something told me he had one.

"What do you have in mind?" I stepped closer to him.

"I want him off the team." Seemed fair to me after he used me to stay on it.

"Sounds good for me. Friends?" I extended my hand, hoping he didn't see the tremble in my fingers.

"You've got yourself a deal, sweetheart." His warm hand closed around mine, and we shook on the grounds of a fake friendship to hurt my ex.

Like a true gentleman, the type you only read about in books, Jaxon walked me to my car, held open the driver's door for me, and then closed it once I was in my seat. I only wished my heart would stop fluttering because as he said...

He wasn't ready for a relationship. Which meant he was certainly not ready for me or this baby.

"Let me get this straight—you chickened out and told your baby daddy you want to be friends?" Scarlett asked, sipping on a glass of red wine. I was back at her place, and we were sitting on the couch, snuggling into a blanket while commercials played on the television.

"I'll admit it didn't go as planned." I cringed at her giggle.

"You don't say. Is he hot, even when you're sober?" Matt turned away from his computer to glare at his wife.

"You do know I'm sitting right here."

"Hush. You know I love you, just like I know you like to watch the cheerleaders at the games." He shook his head, returning his focus to the video game he was playing. "So, on a scale of one to ten, how hot are we talking?"

I wasn't sure if it was the fact that I was pregnant with his baby or that the last time I had seen him it was dark, but he was definitely hot.

"Ten—totally a ten. So, naturally, I'm not sure how we ended up having sex that night. He must have been smashed." Scarlett scoffed and rolled her eyes.

"Right. I hate when you pretend that you're ugly. You're a ten, right, Matt?" He sighed and agreed without really listening to our conversation.

"It doesn't matter. None of that does. He doesn't want a relationship. He wants to get Richard off that team, and I promised to help him." The latest episode of The Bachelor replaced the commercials, and Scarlett quickly paused it.

"Okay, let's pretend like you two aren't going to have hot sex in a few weeks or fall madly in love by the end of this stupid arrangement. You're really going to sell out Richard's secrets and get him kicked from the team? I know he hurt you, but that's not you, Logan." She took a gulp of her wine rather than a sip, and I wished I could the same.

"Don't get involved, Scar," Matt uttered from the corner, shooting his wife a glare.

"Don't tell me what to do with my best friend." She didn't spare him a glance.

"He's not a good guy, so hurting him the way he did to me is deserved. Is it what I had in mind when I went to see Jaxon

tonight? Absolutely not, but I have to get close to him somehow."
She nodded and then downed the rest of her wine.

"What happens when you start showing? You aren't a few weeks pregnant, Logan. You'll have a noticeable bump soon. What are you going to tell him?"

I hadn't thought that far ahead.

Pulling the crumpled list from my back pocket, I glared at the last line. I hated that I wasn't able to tell him.

"I'll tell him I'm pregnant," I uttered, crumpling the paper into a ball and tossing it on the coffee table. Scarlett watched me quietly.

"And when he asks about the father?"

"*If* he asks, Scarlett. Maybe he won't care, and I'll just have to raise this baby on my own." Crossing my arms over my chest, I fought another wave of fucking tears.

She rested her soft hand on my arm. "You'll never have to do this alone. You have me; you always have me, Logan. And something tells me you'll have that very sexy man, too."

"And if I don't have him? If I never work up the courage to tell him that I'm pregnant with his baby?" Fear crept into my tone because as much as I loved my best friend, I never wanted to raise a child alone.

"Don't worry about the what-ifs. Get to know him, let him help you get closure for Richard, and when the time is right, you'll tell him about the little bun in your oven. And if you don't, I will. That's what best friends are for."

I didn't want to worry.

If I had stuck to my ten-year plan, I'd be married right now. I would have a husband. I wouldn't be doing anything alone.

But my plan had gone to hell, and I had to just deal with it.

CHAPTER 10

Jaxon

The sights of Honey Magnolia were welcome after spending the last hour driving through the middle of nowhere. Luke Combs's voice crooned through the speakers of my F-150 as I tapped my fingers along the leather steering wheel.

Nothing had changed in this town since I was here a few months ago. Turning onto the dirt road that led to my parents' ranch, I noticed the newly-painted fences and a new mare grazing in one of the pastures.

Pulling onto the gravel driveway, I shut off the truck and hopped out, inhaling the country air like a starved man. I loved coming home.

Sure, the city life had been fun, and being able to walk a few blocks for food and a good time was all the rage in college, but the older I got, the more I craved privacy and lost interest in the next party.

Kenna's Golden Retriever, King, came running from the barn, tail wagging a mile a minute as he crashed into me, his warm tongue licking any exposed piece of skin he could reach.

"Hey, buddy!" I squatted and pet the big dog, running my fingers through his thick fur.

"And what are you doin' here, cowboy?" McKenna's southern drawl was thick as she stepped out from the barn, her brown hair pulled back into a ponytail, a black tank top tucked into her worn jeans, which were tucked into a pair of old, red boots, the ones my brother had given her a few years ago for their anniversary.

I stood and grinned at her. My sister-in-law was always a sight for sore eyes. We'd grown up together, playing hide and seek in the barn, Cowboys and Indians in the fields, and taking trail rides until our asses didn't belong to us.

My nephew, Douglas, came to stand behind her, wrapping his chubby hands around her leg. "Hey, little man!" I crossed the space between us and pulled him into my arms, throwing him up in the air. His giggles bounced off the barn. "I sure have missed you." He placed his hands on my cheeks, laughter still shaking his small body.

"It's good to have you home, Jax." Kenna gave me a one-armed hug, watching her son with a soft smile.

"It's good to be here. Don't you have your own ranch?" She laughed, playing with Douglas's hair.

"We came to see the colt. Archie's been takin' care of it for your folks." I didn't know about a colt. It had been a long time since we had one on the ranch.

"What's all the noise out here?" Archer walked out of the barn, wiping his hands on his jeans, his black Stetson covering his eyes. "Hey, brother, what brings you home?" He shook my hand and then ruffled his son's hair.

"Needed a break from the city." He took off his hat and rolled his eyes.

"Right. You sure it's not about the fact that we all know you're playin' for the Braves now and you happen to be only two hours away?" Archer had always been able to read me.

"Leave him be, Archie. I'm glad he's here. I missed my baby brother," Kenna teased just as I heard the creek of the front door from the porch.

"Jaxon, is that you? Boy, come greet your momma!" Momma Dexter was possibly the scariest woman I had ever encountered, so handing Douglas back to his father, I bolted for the porch where my momma was standing, hands on her hips.

"Hey, Momma." I bent down to wrap her in a hug.

"It's about time you came back. Your pops and I have been so worried." I rolled my eyes at her dramatics.

"I was home a few months ago," I started to tell her, but from the stern look crossing her features, I wisely snapped my mouth shut.

"Your brothers came back. Don't you think it's your turn, honey? I want to have all my kids in one town again." And this was the very reason why I hadn't come home sooner.

I wasn't ready to give up my life just yet.

"Ma, can we not do this?" I ran a hand through my short hair.

"Come on, he just got here. No need to scare him away." Archer put an arm around my shoulder, ending the dreaded conversation.

We went inside and caught up over lunch. Dad wasn't home, and his absence at the table was a heavy weight that settled on my chest.

I had to get past his reaction, whatever it may be. I just wanted him to be proud of me.

"So, baseball, huh?" Archer asked, his attention on Doug who is in a highchair. My oldest brother still found it a little hard to believe I left football.

I glanced at the women, who were too invested in their own conversation about the upcoming wedding to listen to us.

"It makes sense, man. Being up there in the middle of the field, on the mound. It sets my soul at ease." He nodded thoughtfully, slipping a mouthful of food into his son's mouth while he was distracted with a toy.

"That's how I feel in the shop. Putting a wrench on something just makes everything quiet in my head. Dad understood when I explained. So, he'll understand you deciding to leave football for good. He's not so set in his ways anymore. The kids have softened him."

I sure as hell hoped that was the case, otherwise I would be getting back in my truck and never coming back.

"Dove, I think he's ready for his nap. We ought to be gettin' home," Arch addressed Kenna with her old nickname, the one he came up with for her when we were kids. Those two have always been the perfect little lovebirds, just like real-life turtle doves. The kind that mated for life.

Watching them reminded me of Logan. The ease I had felt having her in my apartment the other night. There was something about her that drew me in.

After cleaning up the dishes, I sat with my momma, catching up on the last few months. She told me about the boys and how she was proud of them for coming home to start families. She hinted at me settling down and asked if there was someone special in my life. Once again, I was reminded of Logan.

What would she think of this place? Would she like my family? Would they like her? Was she worth taking a chance on?

Dad trudged through the front door as the sun started to set, weary from a long day, but his face lit up when he saw me. I stood to greet him, extending my hand to shake, but he bypassed it and pulled me in for a hug.

"Congratulations, my boy!" The strong arms I remembered as a boy were weaker, the skin weathered and wrinkled, but he held me tightly, pouring all his love and approval into me.

That night, I slept in my childhood bed, my feet hang off the edge, and if I turned suddenly, I risked ending up on the floor. But I stared at the walls, the posters of football legends, the trophies on my desk, and wondered what eighteen-year-old me would say if he could see me now.

If things would have happened differently if I knew how my dad was going to react.

When I closed my eyes, Logan infiltrated my thoughts. I could see the curve of her pink lips when she smiled at me, the twinkle in her green eyes. I wanted to get inside of her mind. I wanted to know what diminished her sparkle so I could protect her from it. I needed to know why I couldn't stop thinking about her.

Pulling out my phone, I searched for her name in my contacts. She'd shared her number with me a few days ago, but I'd been scared to text her, to be the first one to contact her.

JAX

Hey, sweetheart.

Instantly, there was a read receipt, and then three dots appeared. I checked the time and cringed at how late it was.

LOGAN

Jaxon?

JAX

How many guys call you sweetheart?

LOGAN

Didn't think you'd ever text me... it's been three days.

JAX

I was trying to decide if you were crazy or not.

LOGAN

And?

JAX

You're crazy beautiful, but not crazy in the head. At least, I think you aren't.

LOGAN

Can't tell if that's a compliment or an insult. You don't know how to talk to women.

JAX

My sisters would agree with you.

LOGAN

Pretty sure the whole female population would agree...

Except the cleat chasers, of course... they think you are the shit.

JAX

Maybe I am?

LOGAN

In your dreams.

JAX

As long as you're there.

LOGAN

I think you're the crazy one.

JAX

I'm visiting my family for a few days. When I get back in town, can we go for coffee?

LOGAN

I don't like coffee.

Chuckling, I shook my head. This girl was something else.

JAX

Tacos?

LOGAN

No, thank you.

JAX

Are you always this hard to please?

LOGAN

I like pizza.

JAX

Then, it's a date.

LOGAN

Thought we were friends?

Fuck, I said no dating. There I went, putting my foot in my damn mouth like a fool.

JAX

Not that kind. A friend date.

LOGAN

Whatever you say, cowboy.

JAX

Night, sweetheart.

LOGAN

Goodnight, Jaxon.

Falling asleep with a big grin on my face, I thought about our friendship date and wondered if I was making a mistake by insisting on friendship.

* * *

RISING EARLY THE NEXT MORNING, I helped Dad on the ranch. Then, I rode over to Archer and Kenna's ranch, taking a worn trail. Dante was there brushing a mare with Alice, his adopted daughter. He spoke calmly to the horse, his voice steady as he brushed through the tangles in her mane.

"You talk to Brook like that, too?" Alice turned to look at me and squealed, dropping her brush to bolt toward me, scaring the mare Dante was working with. He got her under control as I dismounted from my stallion and swung Alice into my arms.

"Ali! What have I told you about screamin' near the horses, honey?" Her face fell, and her bottom lip trembled.

"I'm sorry, Daddy. I got so excited to see Uncle Jax." She wrapped her small arms around my neck and squeezed with all her might. He sighed but smiled at the little girl who had stolen all of our hearts.

"Don't be such a buzzkill, Daddy," I mocked him, to which he rolled his eyes.

"Your turn is comin'. Just you wait." He brought the mare back into the barn and then came out, arms crossed. "I heard from Arch you were in town. Congrats on the contract. How did Dad react?" I set Alice down, and she ran off to go play.

"He hugged me." I scratched the back of my neck and looked up at Dante, a little uncomfortable. His jaw went slack.

"Our dad?" I nodded, walking my horse over to a pail of water. "The man is gettin' soft," Dante said, shaking his head.

He told me about the school he was running, and then about Brooklyn, his wife, and their almost one-year-old, Sawyer.

"Can't believe you're a girl dad." He laughed, looking over at Alice, who was playing with King.

"I thought the same thin', but they're great. I'm their hero, and they are my everythin'."

"Sounds like you are goin' soft." He rolled his eyes and shoved me playfully.

"I can kick your ass any day of the week, Jax. Don't you ever forget that."

Kenna came out her childhood home carrying a tray of fresh lemonade. She gave a smaller glass to Alice, who sipped it quickly and then started running around with Douglas, their laughter surrounding us.

"How nice of you to swin' by." She handed Dante and me each a glass before sipping her own.

"Came to see the ranch. Some of my best memories are here." She looked around the place and smiled.

"Me, too. Arch and I fell in love here," she said wistfully. "You do know your brother is gettin' married in a month? And you haven't RSVP'd."

"Didn't realize that was public knowledge." Dante threw his head back and laughed.

"It is when she's plannin' the weddin', man."

"Right. I'll be there," I said, glancing at the kids who were playing a game of tag.

"And your plus one?" Kenna asked hopefully, her brow raising in curiosity.

Who the hell am I going to bring?

A certain raven-haired beauty crossed my mind. I was sure she wouldn't mind a fun weekend getaway. As friends.

"I'm bringin' a friend."

"Does your friend have a name?" she prodded. Man, she didn't quit.

"It's Logan."

"You can't brin' a guy, Jax!" she whined, and Dante laughed.

"I'm not. Logan's a girl." Kenna's eyes instantly shone with mischief.

"I can't wait to meet her."

I just had to convince her to come first.

CHAPTER 11

Logan

JAXON AND I HAD BEEN TEXTING EACH OTHER A FEW times a day for the last week. How he was flirty through something as emotionless as a text beat me. I tried to remain calm and keep up the easy banter, but the truth was on the tip of my tongue, and I was afraid if we spent any amount of time together, I'd spill my secret, or I'd fall for him.

We were supposed to be meeting in an hour for a 'friend date,' as he called it. My heart skipped a beat when he called it a date but then, it sunk just as quickly when he corrected himself. I blamed the pregnancy hormones because there wasn't any part of me that was ready to jump into a serious relationship, and anything with Jaxon would be *real*.

Dating him would be a horrible idea, especially with the baby coming, and I had to keep reminding myself of that. If I found out he was everything I didn't want in a man, and then I had to raise this child with him, I'd struggle, but even worse, if I found out he was perfect and the only connection I would have was our child, I'd be miserable.

He first wanted to meet for coffee, and right now, the smell of it was making me sick, and I didn't think I could sit in a cafe and stomach the smell while trying to have a serious conversation. If he had asked me three months ago to meet for coffee, I would have jumped at the idea. Cozy cafés were my favorite.

Mexican was off the table, too. Last time I went for tacos with Scarlett, I had nearly thrown up at the table. Pizza was safe—plus, who didn't like a good ole greasy, cheese pizza?

My stomach grumbled at the thought of food. I hadn't had time for my morning snack. Between doctor appointments and collecting my things from the school, I had been running all morning.

Pressing my hand to my stomach, I spoke softly to my little baby, "Are you hungry, little one?" At my appointment this morning, my doctor told me I should start to feel movement, and if I wanted, I could find out the gender.

I declined. I didn't need to know—not without the father there with me. I just wanted this baby to be healthy. The gender didn't matter.

Getting into my car, I immediately locked the doors, turned it on, and blast the heat. Winter had come early this year.

Connecting my phone to the car's Bluetooth, I saw a missed text from Jaxon.

> **JAXON**
> Practice finished early. Are you available now?

> **LOGAN**
> Sure. Where do you want to go?

> **JAXON**
> Gianni's in twenty?

> **LOGAN**
> See you there.

Taking a deep, calming breath, I glanced down at my small stomach, still struggling to believe I was pregnant.

"We're going to see your daddy. Your daddy that doesn't want to date or know about you."

Shifting the car into drive, I quickly got onto the highway and headed for the outskirts of the city. Gianni's had the best pizza in all of Atlanta. Everyone knew that, which meant it was going to be hard to find a table at lunchtime on a Friday.

Somehow, I found a parallel park at the entrance of the small, Italian restaurant. Exiting the car, I just barely managed to dodge a car whizzing by too fast, the wind blowing my hair in disarray.

"Logan!" Jaxon's deep voice shouted from nearby, and suddenly, he was at my back, putting himself between me and the traffic.

He protected me as we edge around my car until we were safely on the sidewalk. I took a steadying breath. *He's a good man.*

"I thought you were gonna get taken out there." He ran a distressed hand through his dark hair, and I watched the muscles in his arm as he moved.

"I should have been looking; I didn't think," I said, walking through the glass door that he was holding open for me. He led me to a booth in the corner, his hand at the small of my back. I wasn't sure if butterflies were wreaking havoc in my stomach or if it was our baby moving, or if I was imagining everything.

He waited for me to sit before sliding into the booth across from me. He glanced around the busy restaurant while I took my sunglasses off and rested them on the corner of the table. He signaled the waiter, asking for menus.

A minute later, a young girl was back, holding two glasses of water, a small metal basket with bread rolls with garlic dipping sauce, and two menus. He thanked her, avoiding her gaze when it lingered a moment too long.

"Are you—" she started to ask, and immediately, he looked at her, shaking his head.

"Please, I'm here having lunch with a friend. I'll sign anything you want; just keep it quiet." Her cheeks flamed and she nodded.

"I'm so sorry. My younger brother is a huge fan. He's been following you for a while. He's on a little league team." Looking at her now, I noticed she was a teenager. Her brother must be very young.

"Bring me a napkin, and I'll send him a note. I appreciate all my fans." She nodded and practically ran to the counter, where she grabbed a napkin and then held out her pen for Jaxon. "His name?"

I watched as he wrote a message on a cheap napkin for someone he didn't know. My heart melted as he signed it off, wishing the boy the best in his career.

"Thank you, Mr. Dexter. What can I get you two to drink?"

We were both content with the water, so she promised to come back in a few minutes to take our order.

"I'm sorry about that. I'm still learning how to handle it." He didn't look at me, instead choosing to focus on the very small menu.

"I think you did just fine. No judgment coming from me." He glanced up, a small smirk tugging at his lips.

"So, what are you in the mood for?"

"I'm happy with a plain old cheese." He shook his head and looked around.

"From here? No way. You have to try the Hawaiian." I cringed.

"You like pineapple on your pizza?"

"You don't?" He laughed, heat creeping up his neck.

"Never tried it. Can't say I like any fruit warm."

"Okay, how about half cheese and half Hawaiian? We can get the best of both worlds." I nodded, pushing the menu to the end of the table, and rested my head on my hand, trying my hardest not to blatantly ogle him.

He was too damn handsome for his own good, and if I stared into his eyes any longer, I was going to tell him everything in the middle of this pizzeria. Wouldn't that just be classy?

Jaxon placed our order and then gulped down his water. "So,

why don't you tell me about that ex of yours? He sure is a piece of work. Not to be rude, but what the hell were you thinkin', datin' him?"

I sipped on my water, thinking about the right answer. What *was* I doing with him?

"I have anxiety, so I make lists, and I made a list of my goals before thirty. Called it my ten-year plan." I watched him, looking for any hint of humor in his expression but saw none. "I dated around in college, couldn't seem to find someone worth settling with, and then, I watched my best friend fall in love and got worried."

"So, you settled for his sorry ass," he added, seeing exactly where I was going with this.

"You could say that. Things were good in the beginning. I saw my future in him, so I moved in, and then shit hit the fan one month at a time. Slowly, I became more of someone to keep his up image instead of someone to share a life with." I played with the wrapper of my straw, rolling it up and then unwinding it and repeating the process.

"So, he used you?" I shrugged, but he shook his head. "The team has a strict no tolerance for a bad image. We have to sign a contract that states we won't be seen partyin', no strin' of women —it goes on. He used you to keep his spot on the team."

I didn't know that.

Richard didn't share a lot about his life, so neither did I. He knew my parents were dead and that I had no one to look out for me, so he took advantage.

"I didn't know," I said as the young girl from before put a metal stand on the table, and then someone put a huge pizza on it.

"Let me know if you two need anything." She waited a beat and then scurried off when Jax nodded at her.

"Coach wants me to take over his position, but the team owner likes him for some reason. Not sure why, but I have to beat him at his own game to get him off the team. "

81

"The team owner is his cousin. That's how he got on the team in the first place. He's only there for the money. He hates the sport." Now, that secret, I did know.

He paused mid-chew, eyes going large. He swallowed quickly just as I was about to have a bite.

"Did you know that's also against the team policy?"

"What?" I hesitated, holding the pizza in front of my mouth.

"Being related to the owner." A flicker of excitement gleamed in his eyes.

"No. I don't know much about the team. I just went to the games in support. My best friend's husband loves the sport, so I get him in with my special tickets."

He nodded, and we polished off the pizza in a few minutes. He managed to convince me to try the Hawaiian, and surprisingly, it did taste good, but I didn't have more than one piece.

The young girl brought us one bill once we finished, and I reached for it, but he handed her his card. Just like that, she was gone again.

"Hey, it was my turn to pay for the pizza." I referenced our first shared pizza, and he shook his head.

"Sorry. No can do, sweetheart. In the south, we're raised to take care of women, even if they are friends." I flushed under his heated gaze, seeing the desire pooling in his eyes as I cross my arms under my chest, pushing up my already swollen boobs up, giving him a nice view of my cleavage.

When the girl came back, she thanked him for the autograph again, wished him luck on the season, and thanked us for coming to her restaurant. "You two are really cute together. I hope to see you two again." I opened my mouth to correct her, but Jaxon just smiled and thanked her, promising to return soon.

He helped me stand, once again placing his hand on the small of my back, and opened the door for me. I was afraid I was going to stumble if he kept this up, and that would be embarrassing. This was certainly not something I'd ever experienced before, and he was going to ruin me for any other man.

Outside, he led me over to a metal bench and gestured for me to join him. Sitting down, he scanned the area and then joined me, his jean-clad leg brushing against mine, warmth seeping into me, and desire setting my blood on fire.

"So, I know we started this whole friendship with other intentions." He was looking up at the blue sky. "But I'd like to really be your friend, Logan. Without Luke here," I was reminded of his friend from the bar that night, "I'm just lost, and I could really benefit from havin' someone I trust in my life."

"I'm not sure if I could come to the games and risk seeing Richard. I had to sneak into our apartment to get my things. I'm not sure how ugly he will get in public." I played with the chain of my necklace, the one my mother gave me.

"Did he hurt you?" His voice broke, and I quickly shake my head.

"Not physically, but verbally and emotionally. And I don't want him to drag your reputation through the mud if you're seen with me."

"Don't worry about me, sweetheart. I'm a big boy. I can take care of myself." He puffed out his chest, but I bit my lip and shook my head.

"Really, Jax," I put my hand on his forearm, and his gaze immediately darted down to where we were touching, "you're just starting out your career with the Braves. Don't let some girl you don't know ruin it."

He placed his big hand over mine, the calluses on his palm rubbing against the top of my hand. "I don't care about the media. And I'm not scared of that asshole. I want to get to know you. I don't want you to be just some girl I don't know."

"Why?" I swallowed, trying to keep my emotions at bay.

"There's somethin' about you, Logan. You keep drawin' me in. You're a goddamn siren, and I'm not ignorin' your song anymore."

Swoon.

Breathe. Inhale. Exhale.

Jaxon Dexter was stealing the breath straight from my lungs.

"And sweetheart, I need a big damn favor." I nodded, not trusting my voice. "Will you be my date to my brother's weddin'?"

What?!

CHAPTER 12
Jaxon

LOGAN'S EMERALD EYES WENT WIDE. SHE BLINKED slowly and inhaled a deep breath. "I can't breathe," she whispered, panic flaring in her eyes.

Was she having another anxiety attack? I wasn't expecting that.

"Uh, shit, okay." I caressed her face and contemplated blowing on her face, but that seemed ridiculous and entirely the wrong thing to do.

She was having an anxiety attack because of everything I just said to her, so I had to distract her. Pressing my lips to hers, I hoped like hell it worked.

Her lips were softer than I remembered. Swiping my tongue along the seam of her plump bottom lip, I sought entrance, but she was frozen beneath my touch. I tenderly bit the soft flesh, and she gasped, lips parting.

I sucked her lip into my mouth, swallowing her moan, and felt her soften against me. I pulled back after a moment and opened my eyes. Her chest was rising and falling rapidly, but she was breathing. Her eyes were electric as they danced across my face. My gaze locked on her tongue when she licked her lips. Her hands were soft on my forearms, her vicious nails biting into my flesh.

"Did—did—" she whispered, her nose brushing against mine, "kiss—you—oh, my God." Her sentence was incoherent but I nodded, pressing another kiss to her lips, and she sighed.

"Yeah, sweetheart, I kissed you, and I want to do it again."

"No, no. I can't think when you do that." She closed her eyes and inhaled a shaky breath. "You just kissed me."

I cracked a grin. "I think we already established that."

"What happened to just being friends?!" she shrieked. I bit my tongue to keep from laughing.

"Changed my mind. Did you miss that part of the conversation? I want to see where this goes." She shook her head, tears pooling in her eyes.

Why is she crying? What did I say?

"But—but you said you aren't that guy, remember?" Her bottom lip trembled. I wanted it between my teeth again. I wanted to take her doubt away.

"I thought I wasn't, but you make me question everythin'."

"This wasn't supposed to happen, Jax. We're supposed to be friends." *Why is she pushing me away?*

"Can you honestly tell me you don't want more? That you don't want me to kiss you? That you don't want to get to know me?" She hesitated, those fucking eyes betraying her.

"Well, no... I can't."

"Then, what's the problem, sweetheart? What are you scared of?" I caressed her face, my thumb brushing her cheek, and her eyes fluttered close.

"I don't want to be alone again. I don't want to be arm candy," she whispered, and my heart splintered at her confession.

"I'm not him, Logan. I can't promise everythin' will work out between us, but I can promise to try. I can give you all of me, and I can promise that you will never be just arm candy to me." She deflated against my touch and my words.

"Okay."

"Okay, so you'll be at my game tomorrow?" Her eyes flew open, wide with panic.

"You must be crazy, Jax!"

"Never said I wasn't, sweetheart. I'll get you and your friends some of my merch to wear, and then, I want you to wait for me there."

"What if he sees?"

I shrugged. "What if he does? I'll be there, and I won't let him hurt you—not a damn hair on your head or a piece of your heart. I protect what's mine."

Her cheeks warmed. "You are crazy, Jaxon."

"Crazy about you," I threw back, and she giggled, rolling her eyes.

"Cheesy, too, I see."

"And about that weddin'—it's next month. I hope you're available?" She nodded and shifted her attention to something over my shoulder.

"We have company, Jax," she whispered, and I saw the glint of the camera lenses from the bushes behind me.

I hate the paparazzi.

"Let me walk you to your car," I stood and offered her my hand, which she took. I led her to her car, watching the traffic so we both didn't get run over. Then, I held open the driver's side door for her.

"You really don't have to do that. I could've just slipped in." I shook my head as she slid into her seat. Leaning into the car, I pressed a kiss to her cheek.

"Wasn't raised that way. Now, buckle up and drive safe. I'll see you tomorrow." She nodded, and then, I closed the door and jogged down the road to where I parallel-parked my truck. I waited for her to merge into traffic, and then did the same, making sure I wasn't being followed as I headed for my apartment.

Once I was safely in my apartment, I shot her a text.

JAX

Did you make it home?

LOGAN

Just pulled into the driveway. Thank you for lunch.

JAX

Where is home?

LOGAN

With my best friend until I can find something.

JAX

Can you meet me an hour before the game tomorrow for the merch?

LOGAN

Only if you can get us good seats.

JAX

Done.

* * *

THE NEXT DAY, I was waiting in the team parking lot for my agent to bring Logan and her friends here. When I saw her, her black hair pulled back into a braid, wearing a pair of jeans and a loose V-neck with a pair of white Converse, I was sure my knees were going to give out on me. *She's perfect.*

She smiled nervously as her best friend and husband followed behind her. The blonde walked straight up to me and stuck out her hand. "Scarlett Humphrey, Logan's best friend. Nice to meet you, Jaxon." Logan cringed out of the corner of my eye, but I shook Scarlett's hand and then her husband's, Matt, who apologized for his brazen wife.

"Honestly, Scar, did you not listen to a word I said in the car?" Logan complained, glaring at her best friend.

"Since when do I listen to you or Matt? I do whatever I want, when I want. Now, Jaxon, what do you have for us to wear?"

I like this one.

My agent handed out shirts with my number 99 printed in bold letters and my last name. Then, he handed out hats with my number that Logan secured to her head after throwing the shirt on.

She looked good with my name on her. After fixing her hair, she smiles at me, her green eyes brighter today and rimmed with black.

"You look good, sweetheart." I placed my hands on her waist and drew her closer to me.

"Are you going to pitch today?" she asked, tilting her head up.

"Second half. Coach insisted. My agent is going to take you to your seats, and then, I'll see you after the game—outside the lockers?" A flicker of uncertainty passed through her eyes, but her best friend was there to soothe her.

"She'll be there. I'll make sure of it. Thank you for all of this. We're huge fans. Well, he is." She pointed behind her at her husband, who grinned sheepishly.

I placed a quick kiss on Logan's cheek and then headed out, waving at Scarlett and Matt. She was safe with them, and I knew I don't have to worry about Richard with that fiery friend.

It was my first game with the team, and Richard was pissed about sharing the mound. But Coach's instructions out-ruled his cousin. When it was finally my turn to take the field, I looked over to where I saved seats for Logan and her friends. She was smiling and waving just like every other fan on the ground, but it was different coming from her.

I stepped up the mound. My number was announced and then my name. The announcer told the stadium my back story, and then, it was go-time.

Inhale.

I raised my leg. I had a lot to prove today. Too many people to please. I made my mind go blank and let the peace wash over me, while I did what I loved.

Exhale.

And I threw the ball.

* * *

WE WON, and I threw another three-digit mile-per-hour pitch. My name was screamed by fans, but I only had eyes for Logan, who was jumping up and down on her feet after the announcer informed everyone about another 105 mile-per-hour pitch.

My spot on this team had just become solidified.

I showered quickly, wanting to get out of here before Richard, needing to get to Logan first, who I knew was already nervous.

Everyone wanted to stop and congratulate me, and I tried to avoid being rude. But Richard was already slipping out as the catcher slapped me on the back in congratulations.

I rushed out after him and saw Logan standing there, Scarlett at her side. Logan's eyes were bouncing around, searching for me in the crowd. I spotted Richard ahead, making his way toward my girl.

I pushed past fans and cleat chasers until I was running past him. Logan saw him and took a step back, but then, her eyes shifted to mine, and she relaxed.

I kept my promises.

I stopped just in front of her, my sneakers squeaking against the concrete. I dropped my bag, cupped her face with both hands, and kissed her in front of everyone.

Her hands wrapped around mine, and she sighed into the kiss. Pulling back, I brushed my nose to hers. "I promised you I wouldn't let him hurt you."

"I know. I know," she whispered.

"Well, that was hot," Scarlett said from my side.

"You moved on real fast, babe," Richard's nasally voice interrupted our moment. "And here I thought you were faithful to me." He grinned as the paparazzi zero in on us, coming closer like the hungry vultures they were.

Logan melted into my chest, and I held her tightly to me.

"I was faithful to you. You cheated on me!" she cried, hiding her face in my neck.

"Never saw you kiss me like that, Logan," he spat, anger lacing every venomous word.

"That's what happens when a real man comes in and shows her what she's been missin'." Scarlett giggled and started to speak, but she was pulled away—by Matt, I presumed.

"First, you come for my position, and now, my girl. You're a dead man walking, Dexter. Your brother might have been some hot-shot, but he doesn't have the same connections that I do." There was a glint in his eye—a threat.

"At least I play by the rules. Wonder what the league would think about your relationship with the team owner." His eyes shot toward Logan, hatred shining in them.

"You keep your fucking mouth shut, whore." I saw red, but Logan's grip on my shirt grounded me. I wouldn't rise to his bait.

"Stay away from us—from Logan—Balmer, or I'll go straight to the league." I reached down for my duffle and swung it onto my shoulder. Putting my arm around Logan's shoulders, I led her out of the stadium toward my truck.

"Holy shit!" Scarlett squealed. "I can see the headlines now!"

"Not now, Scar," Logan weakly mumbled, and I finally noticed just how pale she looked.

"Do you need some water?" I pulled a bottle from my bag and handed it to her, which she greedily gulped.

"We're gonna head home. Great game, man!" Matt pulled his wife away, who glared at him.

"Seriously, Matt, I want to stick around. What if there's more drama?" He shook his head and continued to lead her away.

At my truck, I helped Logan into the passenger seat. She was quiet and ashen, her eyes too big. Dumping my bag into the back-seat, I quickly rounded the hood and hopped into the driver's seat.

After inserting the key and switching the truck on, I turned to her. "I'm sorry. I should have listened to you. I tried to get to you sooner, but I couldn't." She shook her head and reached for me with a shaky hand.

"You did get to me, Jax. You protected me. But your name is going to be all over the tabloids, the headlines!" I linked our fingers together and brought her hand to my lips.

"Let them talk, sweetheart. I don't care." Her eyes shone in the darkness of the cab, and I swore I saw a lone tear roll down her cheek. But then, I blinked, and it was gone.

"You're crazy," she whispered.

"About you," I replied, and she giggled.

Everything was just the way it was meant to be.

CHAPTER 13

Logan

IT HAD BEEN A WHOLE MONTH SINCE JAXON AND I started dating—a whole thirty days of keeping the biggest secret from him. And every day, the guilt ate away at another piece of me.

"I don't know why you haven't told him already. You know he's the sweetest man on the planet, and he's had your back from the first moment you met." Scarlett and I were at a dress shop, where we were struggling to find something that concealed my bump and matched the navy color scheme.

"You know why. What do you think about this one?" I held up the only reasonable option, and she scrunched her nose.

"Do you want to look like a whale?" Rolling my eyes, I put the dress back on the rack. "How do you get out of sex?" I shrugged.

"He hasn't asked." She paused.

"You must be joking. That hot, extremely sexy, baseball-playing cowboy with the most perfect ass I've ever seen hasn't asked or even *attempted* to have sex with you in a whole month?" I nodded and held up another dress for her, which she shook her head at.

"I think he's been waiting to introduce me to his family." Which I was insanely nervous about. Richard never introduced me

93

to his family, and I never thought anything of it, but now that someone wanted me to meet their family, I was basically one breath away from an anxiety attack.

"That's good and bad news. Do you have to wear navy? Look at this black one." I shook my head.

"You can't wear black to a wedding. That's bad luck." She scoffed and rolled her eyes.

"That's bullshit. Plenty of people wore black to mine, and look at me and Matt. I think we should head to a maternity shop. We aren't going to find anything here." I knew she was right, but maternity clothes always put emphasis on the bump, and I didn't want him to find out this weekend.

"Maybe I should wear a pantsuit instead. I mean, I'm only five months. I can still hide it, right?" I glanced at a mirror, where I could see my small bump protruding.

"Why are you trying to hide your perfect little baby, Logan? I wish I had one. I'd walk around topless so everyone could see." Surprising coming from the woman who didn't like kids. If I was in her boat, I'd probably be doing the same thing, but I wasn't, and she would never understand. She was *married*. I was not.

"How far is the maternity store? He's going to pick me up in two hours." She pulled it up on the GPS on her phone, and we quickly got in her car and arrived at the nearest one.

"I can't believe you waited until the last minute to get a dress. You are totally crazy. Also, I can't believe he invited you to a wedding the same day he decided he wanted to date you. He's crazy about you. You're basically made for each other," Scarlett gushed as she held open the door for me. A bell went off, announcing our arrival into the small boutique.

An hour later, we found a navy dress with long sleeves that didn't emphasis my belly. If anything, it hid it. We then rushed home and threw everything I might need into the suitcase for the weekend trip. She threw in some sexy lingerie just in case, which made me roll my eyes, and then, we waited for Jaxon.

"You do know I won't be using that. Not even in the slightest," I told her, but she just grinned.

"Maybe that's how you should tell him. I really don't think he'll be mad. Shocked, yes, but never mad." Matt walked into the kitchen and threw his wife the side eye.

"Don't push her, Scar. If she doesn't want to tell him until the day she delivers, then so be it."

"I swear, you are the biggest buzzkill," Scarlett whined but walked around the kitchen counter to give him a kiss. "Good thing I love you so much."

"I love you more." He kissed the top of her head and wrapped his arm around her. He was always trying to keep her in place, out of kindness and love, because he had seen her burned before from giving advice. He had been witness to the fights between her sisters and her mother—even her and me.

He was the peacekeeper.

A knock sounded at the door a minute later, and Scarlett lit up, like it was her boyfriend and not mine. "Have fun. Do everything I would do." She hugged me tightly and then whispered something to my belly. Once she left with Matt to give me some privacy, I swung open the door and smiled at the breathtaking, handsome man waiting on the other side.

"You are a sight for sore eyes." He cracked a lopsided grin, and my heart skipped a beat at the lame line.

"It's only been one day," I whispered, closing the distance between us. Leaning up on my toes, I pressed a quick, soft kiss to his stubble. He'd been growing a beard for the last two weeks, and I loved everything about it.

"Doesn't matter. I can't get enough of you, sweetheart." He reached behind me for my suitcase and brushed his lips against mine, stealing my breath away.

How after a month of kissing him, he could still make my heart race and my lungs struggle for air was beyond me.

"Come on. Get in the truck. We've got to get there for the

rehearsal dinner. My damn sister-in-law, Kenna, is being real annoyin' about this whole weekend." He'd already explained his entire family tree, from his three older brothers to their wives and children. He showed me pictures, so I wouldn't look like a fool. I was ready to be part of a family again, even if it wasn't really mine.

An hour into the drive, he was whistling along to Luke Combs, an artist I noticed he listened to a lot. "Where are your parents?" I had been wondering when he was going to ask. I didn't like to advertise the information, and I didn't like the pitying looks that followed.

"They both died." He jerked his head in my direction, the car swerving into the other lane for a brief moment.

"Baby, why didn't you tell me sooner?" I fingered the chain around my neck I always wore while I searched for the right answer.

"I wanted you to think I was perfect—with the family and everything. I just get tired of everyone looking at me like I'm broken because of it." He reached for me, his fingers latching onto my bouncing knee, his warmth sinking through the thick fabric of my jeans.

"With or without parents, you're pretty damn perfect to me, sweetheart." I waited for him to ask how they passed, just like everyone else, but after two songs played, I decided to volunteer the information for once.

"My dad died from a complication with surgery. It was a freak accident, and it happened when I was in middle school. And my mom..." My voice shook. Her death had rattled me to the bone. "She was diagnosed with breast cancer when I was very young, and eventually, it spread everywhere. The chemo was only hurting her. A few weeks after my 18th birthday, she told me she couldn't hold on any longer." His grip tightened, and the tears I'd fought every time I told someone slowly rolled down my cheeks.

"I'm sorry. I'm so sorry you had to go through that so young. I wish I could have been there." His words struck a chord. No one had ever said that. They always offered condolences but never wished to be there.

Scarlett had been there. She had held me up at the funeral, wiped away every tear, and forced me to live again when all I wanted to do was to die. She was more my sister than my best friend.

"Sometimes, we get dealt a rough hand in life, but then, we all have two hands." I wasn't following him. I knew he meant well, but I was clueless.

"Jax, I don't understand." He linked his fingers through mine.

"I'm offering you the other hand, sweetheart. I can't promise it'll always be perfect, but I can promise I ain't goin' anywhere. I don't think I could ever leave you."

Was it possible to fall in love in such a short amount of time? *Yes. It most certainly was.*

And I was going to ruin everything with this secret.

* * *

DRIVING INTO HIS HOMETOWN, I noticed the streets were lined with Magnolia trees, and I finally understood the name. It was like stepping into a time capsule as we drove through downtown, where I watched people greet one another. I saw the historic buildings and wondered what it must have been like growing up here.

"Why did you leave?" I asked, almost pressing my nose to the glass of his window in pure excitement.

"Couldn't play ball here. All my brothers left chasin' big dreams, and somehow, they've all ended up back where they started." He turned the truck onto a dirt road, and I saw his family's name on a large sign.

"Do you plan on doing the same?" I found the courage to ask.

"Depends, I guess." I caught his shrug out of the corner of my eye. "You told me once you like lists. What was your plan?"

"Find love. Get married. Buy a house, preferably on the water, with lots of land for all the kids and dogs I want. Rescue a dog. Fall pregnant with the man of my dreams. And raise a beautiful family." I recited the list I had memorized a long time ago.

"In that order?" he questioned, driving past a big house, his tires crunching under the gravel.

"Exactly like that."

"And when did you make that list?"

"After my mom died. I didn't want to live anymore either, so Scarlett showed me by making lists every day that there was a life worth living, and then, I made my ten-year plan. By now, I was supposed to have two kids, a dog, and a husband. I was supposed to have it all." He stopped in front of a tiny log cabin.

"You can keep your list, but who says it has to be in that order?" Shifting the truck into park, he shut it off and turned his attention to me.

"Me, of course." He shook his head with a chuckle.

"I can help you check some of those things off your list," he said, opening his door and hopping out. I waited for him to get to my door to open it, something I learned he loved to do.

While he rounded the hood, I studied him, trying to figure him out. Here, he was no longer the city boy I'd come to love. And what the hell did he mean he could help me check some of the things off my list?

"Humor me. How are you going to check off things on my list?" I wanted to tell him he had already done that, but I feared now wasn't the right time, not when things were so perfect between us.

"I could make you fall in love with me." My heart stopped, and I stumbled into him as he led me into the cabin, twisting open the knob on the bright red front door.

"Jaxon," I whispered his name, unable to focus on anything other than him.

"Tell me you aren't already fallin', sweetheart." He pressed me against the front door, cradling my face in his large, calloused hands.

"I can't do that," I whispered.

"Then, it's quite simple. I'll be the man to check everythin' off that list, one by one."

I can't breathe.

And for the first time, I wasn't having an anxiety attack. Jaxon Dexter had officially stolen my breath away.

"I've been waitin' a long time to bring you here," he said, pulling me off the door to show me the small, cozy cabin.

"What do you mean?"

"Each of my brothers brought their girls here, and this is where they fell in love. Now, it's my turn, and you're the woman I want." My eyes scanned the small space, the lounge set in front of a flat-screen, the open layout kitchen, a tiny table for two, and then one door that led to another room.

"There's only one room," I said, turning back to him.

"It's not like we haven't shared a bed before, sweetheart."

I am screwed.

There's no way I can hide the baby from him while sharing a bed.

CHAPTER 14

Jaxon

LOGAN'S EMERALD EYES WERE WIDE AS SHE GLANCED between me and the cabin. I wasn't sure where her sudden panic came from. We'd shared a bed that night all those months ago, and it hadn't been a problem then. But then again, we'd been drunk.

We could stay in my parents' house, but I wanted the privacy.

I wanted to be alone with her.

I wanted to see her first thing in the morning when her guard was down and right before going to bed at night.

Scratching the back of my head, I let my eyes skim her beautiful body. God, she was a fucking knockout in a pair of leggings and an over-sized sweater.

"We can stay in the house, if you want? My parents have extra rooms," I offered, wanting her to be comfortable more than I wanted to be selfish. She finally looked at me, her eyes softening. "But I really wanted to bring you here." I closed the small space between us, my hands finding her waist, fingers slipping beneath her sweater and pressing into her warm skin.

She sighed into my hold, leaning her head forward. "Why?" she whispered. Her hair tickled my chin, and I pulled her closer, hating any inch of space between us.

"Because I want to share a bed with you, sweetheart."

"Do you tell all the girls that? You bring them all here to your little love shack?" she teased, but I heard a hint of fear in her tone.

This wasn't meant to be a love shack. We'd originally built it for my oldest brother to live in after he tore his ACL, ending his football career. When his childhood sweetheart came back into town and moved in with him, he started the love shack tradition.

They had fallen in love and then moved into her parents' ranch home to start their own family. A year later, my other brother, Dante, moved in and fell for a woman running from her husband. He bought them a big piece of land down the road, where they lived with her toddler and then had their own child shortly after.

And last year, Gage had come home and moved in here, wanting to find his fresh start. Luckily for him, his high school sweetheart hadn't been able to move on either, and those two were getting married tomorrow.

"We can stay here, but no funny business, sir." She poked my chest and stepped away from me, going to look around.

"No promises, sweetheart." She looked at me over her shoulder, a teasing grin lighting up her face. I was falling for her—hook, line, and sinker.

* * *

IN THE CAB of my truck an hour later, we were driving the down the dirt road that led to Kenna and Archer's ranch, where the rehearsal dinner was being held.

Logan's knees were knocking together with nerves, and she was biting her nails, looking out the window in awe at the scenery. Gently taking her hand away from her mouth, I linked our fingers.

"No need to be nervous. They will love you." She shook her head and continued to gaze out the window.

"I've never met someone's family before," Logan finally mumbled when I shifted the truck into park. The whole town must be here from the looks of it, and all I could feel was Logan's nerves and panic as it bounced around the cab of the truck.

"Trust me. They are goin' to be so damn thrilled I'm bringin' a girl home that they won't be judgin' you, sweetheart." I brought her hand to my lips and kissed her soft skin.

"I just..." She hesitated, looking at me and then through the windshield at all the people mingling under the tent in the distance. "I need them to like me."

"Trust me, you'll be wishin' they didn't because they might never let us leave." A small smile tugged at her red lips, and I fought every urge to smear that goddamn lipstick and kiss her.

"Then, I hope they hold us hostage." The softest giggle filled the cab, and I watched some of the nerves disappear from her eyes.

Hopping out of the truck, I jogged around the hood, needing to get her in my arms. She had already opened the door and was trying to stand on the gravel in the pair of heeled boots she paired with jeans and a white sweater, looking like a damn angel, sent here as my redemption.

"You're the most beautiful woman I've ever seen, sweetheart." I grabbed her hips, fingers sinking into her stiff jeans. "But if you open that door again, there'll be consequences."

She blushed and grinned so hard, I caught the briefest hint of a dimple in her cheek again.

"We're already sharing a bed, cowboy. No need to butter me up." She rested her hand over my heart, and I wondered if she could feel it beating double time.

Does she know that it beats for her?

"In case you didn't know, sweetheart, I'm crazy about you. The way you look is just the cherry on top. You have me fallin' damn hard. I hope you can catch me."

Red crept up her neck and into her cheeks. Her lips fell open in the softest gasp I had ever heard.

"Jax, you can't mean that. We hardly know each other." Her

hand found the edge of my jacket, her fingers curling into the material, pulling us closer together.

I wondered if she notices that we always gravitated closer, that we both were falling.

"I mean every damn word, Logan." I kissed the corner of her lips, and she moaned.

"Then, who is gonna catch me?" she whispered, standing on her toes so that her nose brushed mine.

It took every muscle in my body to stay still, to stop myself from kissing her. She had warned me back at the cabin not to ruin her lipstick. She threatened to sleep on the couch if I ruined the makeup she spent nearly an hour perfecting.

"I will. I'll always catch you, sweetheart. You never have to worry about gettin' hurt when I'm around. I've got your back." There was a new light in her eyes, and I wished more than anything I could capture this moment, that I could save the happiness that shone in her eyes so I could take it all in, not even daring to breathe.

"We're going to be late, and then, I'll look really bad," she whispered, nodding her head toward the tent, but I didn't care.

"They won't notice." I spoke too soon because suddenly, a tiny body barreled straight into us, and I barely have a chance to steady Logan and catch the wiggling body that was exploding in giggles.

"Uncle Jax! You're finally here!" Alice screamed in pure excitement. I hoisted her up into my arms, and she threw her tiny arms around my neck, squeezing with all her might. "I missed you so much. Did you know that?" She peppered kisses all over my cheek. Out of the corner of my eye, I saw Logan covering her laughter.

"I missed you, too, Ali bug."

She swiveled around in my arms, and her eyes scanned over Logan. "Who is your pretty friend?" she whispered loud enough for Logan to hear. "Do you think she likes horses? What about babies? She can have Sawyer."

I shook my head at the outspoken child and let Logan answer, knowing she adored kids. "Hey, Ali. I'm Logan. I've heard so much about you."

Alice looked between the two of us, raising a blonde brow. "Of course, you have. I'm Uncle Jax's favorite niece. Did he tell you that?" She pressed another wet kiss to my cheek.

"I have two nieces, Alice, and you're both my favorite." She glared at me, looking so much like her mother.

"Right, so are you more than friends like my mommy and daddy?" She winked at Logan, who stifled another laugh. "I might have overheard Daddy telling Mommy to 'be nice'." She put little air quotes around the word. "I dunno why he said it like Mommy isn't nice."

Shaking my head at her, I put her on my hip and wrapped my arm around Logan, leading her to the tent.

"I remember your mommy not always being so nice," I told her, and she gasped.

"No way! Tell me more!" She wrapped her feet around my waist, anchoring herself to me.

"Maybe another time. I have to introduce Logan to everyone, honey."

"My daddy calls Mommy his honeybee. Did you know that?" She was looking at Logan now, who smiled sweetly.

"I did not. That's so sweet. Do you know why?" Alice nodded her head, her curls bouncing with the quick movement.

"Because she's sweet as honey and annoyin' as a bee. At least, that's what Daddy says." I choked on my laughter because it sounded exactly like something my brother would say.

I put her down, and she waved at us as she ran off, calling for Douglas, who was playing with King, throwing the Golden Retriever a ball as far as he could.

"I love her." Logan sighed, watching wistfully.

Does she want kids, too?

Do I want kids?

Am I ready to settle down with her?

At the tent, we ran into my brothers first. All three of them were standing in the corner hiding, nursing beers like we hadn't all thrown our names away at bars or after parties. Things were different now. They were all family men now, fathers—or soon to be, in Gage's case.

"He brought the girl!" Dante cheered, clinking his beer with Gage, who smirked.

"Whatever. Logan, these are my dipshit brothers. Please excuse their lack of manners. They were raised in the south." She grinned, nervousness flickering in her eyes, but it quickly disappeared when Archer pulled her in for a hug.

"It's so good to meet the one who finally tamed him. Kudos to you, Logan. And don't forget you were raised in the same house, asshole." He shoved my chest, and I took a staggering step back, watching as Dante and Gage introduced themselves and made my girl feel at ease amongst a sea of strangers.

I love my family.

"Let me grab, Kenna. She's runnin' around here somewhere. Looks like a chicken without a head," he muttered the last bit while searching for his wife, who was behind him.

"You talkin' about me again, Archie?" She sauntered over, a glass of champagne sparkling in her grasp, her green eyes slitted in a glare.

"Only good things, dove." She rolled her eyes and stepped away from Archer to hug Logan, who was watching everything with wide eyes.

"It's so nice to meet you, honey. I'm McKenna, but please call me Kenna. I'm married to this idiot." She jabbed a finger behind her at Archer, who grinned, not the least bit insulted.

"You say it like it's a bad thin'."

"Sometimes, it is." Kenna was smiling from ear to ear despite the jab. "Come on. Let me introduce you to the rest of the family. They are dyin' to meet you!" She grabbed Logan by the elbow and whisked her away, leaving me with my very curious brothers.

"She the one?" Gage asked, handing me a beer, which I gratefully took. I needed something to take the edge off my nerves.

"Yup. Wouldn't have brought her if she wasn't." He nodded, and Archer's stupid grin widened.

"You movin' back home, then?" Everyone wanted me back in Honey Magnolia, but I wasn't ready.

"I have the team. Not makin' a two-hour commute every day." He and Dante nodded in understanding.

"What are you goin' to do after the team? You can't play ball forever." Dante knew firsthand the physical tolls of playing at a professional level.

"I'll move back and coach or somethin'. Can't see myself runnin' a farm." I shrugged, looking for Logan, who was surrounded by Kenna, Brooklyn, and Carter. She was smiling, her body no longer tense.

They loved her, just like I promised. So far, I had yet to break one, and I didn't plan on breaking one anytime soon.

I wanted her to know she wasn't ever goin' to be alone again—not with me.

CHAPTER 15
Logan

Jaxon's family was everything I had expected and more. His sisters-in-law were sweet, all three of them. His brothers were just as kind, and his parents were downright perfect.

It was everything I didn't have, and everything I could have hoped for our baby.

"We are dyin' to know how you two met," Carter, the bride-to-be, said, sipping on a sparkling flute of champagne.

Hesitating, I looked into the eyes of each woman, and somehow, I just knew that they wouldn't judge me. They all adored Jaxon and only wanted the best for him, which was what I wanted for him, too.

"At a bar, actually." I looked away from their curious gazes to watch Jaxon with his brothers, his head thrown back with laughter.

The dinner had ended an hour ago. All the other guests had left, and we'd moved into Kenna and Archer's large home. We'd taken over their cozy lounge, while the kids slept upstairs and the men sat in the kitchen.

"I totally see where this is going." Brooklyn grinned, holding her sleeping baby in her arms. "He was all handsome and dazzling with that grin of his, and you ended up in his bed, right?"

Kenna laughed, and Carter blushed with a giggle.

"Well, kinda, yeah." Their laughter was infectious, and soon, the men were leaning over the back of the sofa to pry the information out of their wives.

"You're tellin' me you met this beautiful woman, who's willin' to put up with you, in a bar?" Dante shook his head, plopping down on the sofa next to his wife. Brooklyn immediately sank into his chest and adjusted their sleeping baby in her arms.

"Hard to believe, I know, but she needed me." Jax shrugged, coming to sit beside me. "I was the perfect distraction from her ex." He winked, and the woman all rolled their eyes.

"How on Earth do you put up with his ego?" Carter whispered loud enough for him to hear. "I can barely handle Gage's."

Kenna and Brooklyn joined in, agreeing that their husbands had bigger-than-average egos, and in that moment, we become lifelong friends.

"Alright, not to end our fun, but last time I checked, there is a weddin' tomorrow, and I need some sleep." Brooklyn waited for Dante to stand and then handed over a still-sleeping Sawyer.

"You can leave, Ali. I'm sure she and Dougie are fast asleep." Kenna stood with a yawn and hugged Brooke.

"So, we'll all be back here in..." Gage squinted at his watch, and then, his eyes widened, "Am I seein' this right?"

"Yeah, man. It's two A.M. Blame the women for the lack of sleep." Archer slapped his younger brother on the back and then wrapped his arms around Kenna, pulling her to his chest and resting his chin on her shoulder.

We all quickly said our goodbyes and then exited the beautiful home.

Jax took my hand and led us to his truck, where we made the short trip home. Then, I was faced with the hardest part of the night.

"You can take the bathroom first; I'll get the fire goin'. How about some hot chocolate?" Jax stood awkwardly in the kitchen, his hand scratching his neck as his eyes skimmed over me.

My mouth went dry from the desire pooling in his heated gaze. I wanted him. I needed him to rip my clothes off right here, right now.

"Sweetheart?" Jax's husky voice snapped me out of my fantasy, and I shook my head, my cheeks flushing as I took a step back.

"Are you sure?" He nodded, crossing his arms over his chest. "And I'd love a hot chocolate." A lopsided grin tugged at his beautiful face, and I was frozen in the moment, wishing it would never end.

The bathroom was just as cozy as the rest of the house, and I fell in love with the waterfall shower head when it eases every knot of tension from my body.

I spent the ten-minute shower convincing myself to tell Jaxon before I got in that bed, but I was afraid to lose what we had.

Even though it was all built on a lie, I didn't want it to ever end.

I wanted him to look at me like I was his purpose for the rest of my life. I wanted to be loved by him, and I wanted our child to be loved by him.

I stared at my reflection in the mirror, the small bump where our baby was growing, my swollen breasts, electric eyes, and flushed cheeks. *I have to do this.*

Throwing on the least sexy pair of pajamas I owned, I put my big robe on over it, hoping to conceal the baby until he had showered.

Brushing my wet hair, I exited the bathroom, my entire body shaking with nerves when I saw him sitting on the bed, looking more irresistible than that night we shared together.

"What's wrong?" His deep voice pulled me out of visions from that night, the way his big hands felt on my skin, how his voice sounded while he whispered in my ear.

"Nothing. Your turn, cowboy." He grinned, and the butterflies that were already going crazy in my stomach intensified.

I was just about to sit on the floor and dry my hair when he stopped and suddenly caged me in against the wall. The muscles in his biceps and forearms held me hostage as his nose skimmed along my jaw. I forgot to breathe when the tip of his tongue tasted my skin.

He kissed along my jaw and then nibbled on my earlobe. My breaths came out in uneven pants, and I used every ounce of strength to keep standing.

"Jax," I moaned, dropping the hair dryer and sinking one hand into his hair and the other into his shirt to pull him closer.

He pulled away slowly, his eyes dark, his lips pink, and his hair in disarray from my fingers. The breath was sucked straight from my lungs at the sight of him.

"Get into bed, sweetheart. I won't be long." He stepped into the bathroom and then paused. "No fallin' asleep now. I'm not finished with you yet." I nodded because I couldn't remember how to speak.

I used the little strength I had left to dry my hair and then take my vitamins before bed. I saw the hot chocolate on the bedside table and sipped the hot drink while I waited in bed, just like he asked me to.

When he finally exited the bathroom after a long ten minutes, I was a mess. I couldn't remember the words I had rehearsed in the shower, and I certainly couldn't think straight when he walked out shirtless, steam billowing out behind him.

"I almost expected to find you on the couch," he joked, throwing his dirty clothes into his suitcase and then plugging his phone into the charger next to *his side* of the bed. I gulped, searching for the right answer. But I couldn't seem to find it in time because he flipped the lights, bathing us in darkness except for a sliver of moonlight that filtered in from a gap in the curtain.

He slid into the bed, and when the mattress dipped, I fought the urge to throw myself at him. "What's got you so stiff?" His voice was even sexier in the darkness. How was that possible?

"I—I have to tell you something, Jax." He closed the space between us and crawled over me. I pressed my back flat to the mattress, hoping he didn't feel the baby.

"Can it wait? I have a lot of missed time to make up with you." He softly kissed my jaw and then the corner of my lips.

What am I going to tell him again?

My fingers threaded into his short hair, tugging him closer. I didn't want this to end.

"I'm pregnant." And he stilled, his body tensing above mine.

"What do you mean?" He started to sit up, and my fingers lost their grip and fell to my stomach. In the darkness, I couldn't see his reaction, but he had pulled away from me, which was a bad sign. Dread curled in my gut.

It was all over.

"It's yours. It's why I came to find you, but I've been too scared to tell you. Please don't hate me or the baby. Please, Jax." Tears were rolling down my cheeks faster than I could spit the story out. My chest was rising and falling too fast, and suddenly, it became hard to breathe.

"Breathe, Logan. Breathe, sweetheart." His hands cupped my face, his body pressing into mine while I fought the panic attack.

"I'm sorry. I'm so sorry. I'm sorry," I blubbered, but he placed a finger on my wet lips.

"Stop apologizing," he whispered, wiping away my warm tears as they rolled down my cheeks. "Are you sure it's mine?"

"You're the only person I've slept with this year," I whispered in the thick silence.

"Fuck. Okay, it's definitely mine. You're pregnant with my baby."

Using one of the counting techniques I had learned to cope with the anxiety attacks, I slowly got my breathing under control while Jax tried to gather his thoughts.

"I'll take the couch so you can process this." I started to sit up, but his hand around my face lowered to my hips, pressing me into the bed.

"You aren't goin' anywhere, Logan." I was between his strong legs, his warm hands pressing into my skin, and I didn't want to be anywhere else. "You must be..." he goes quiet, trying to do math.

"Five months," I whispered, and his hold tightened.

"You waited that long to tell me? Did you think I was a monster you couldn't come to?" Pain laced every word, and I shook my head, my hands rising to cup his face.

"I found out a few days before I came to you. You aren't a monster, Jax. You are so far from it. I got to know you, and then, I fell for you. And the thought of you pushing me away after falling for you was—is—unbearable, but I can't hide this from you." His hands left my hips and came to rest on my stomach.

There was a tiny flutter when the baby kicked, and I cried. They knew daddy was here. "Why are you cryin'? I'm not pushin' you away. I can't lose you either." His confession made the tears come quicker.

"Can you feel that?" I moved his hand right where the baby was kicking, and he stilled.

"Is that..."

"I know it's a lot, Jax. I know you weren't ready for a relationship or to settle down, so I understand if—" Jaxon closed the space between us, pressing his lips to mine.

"I thought I wasn't ready, Logan, but I was ready for you the moment you came into my life. So, you better not be comin' up with some shared custody plan. I want all of it with you. I just wish it had happened differently."

"Different how?"

"I wish I could have helped you with that checklist. But don't worry. Now that I know about it, you can be damn sure I'll do my best to check everythin' off that list, sweetheart." My heart skipped a beat because no one had ever understood my obsessive need to check off lists.

"Are you saying what I think you are?"

"If you're askin' if I love you, then the answer is yes. I was going to tell you after a round of some mindblowin' sex, but since you're lyin' beneath me, carryin' my child, it seems like a fittin' time, don't you think?"

"I think I've been in love with you since that night." I brushed my nose along his, our lips so close, I could taste his warm breath.

"I think you deserve some lovin', sweetheart. I've shown you once before, but I think you need to be reminded of how a cowboy takes care of their woman." If I hadn't been lying down already, I'd have fallen to my feet.

"You're not mad?" I whispered, threading my fingers through his hair once again.

"Not even a little. You've given me everythin' I didn't know I needed in just one night. I couldn't be happier, Logan."

CHAPTER 16

Jaxon

I WAS GOING TO BE A FATHER.

Logan's warm, soft, even breaths brushed against my chest as she slept soundly. Her hair tickled my jaw, but I couldn't find it in me to move it away.

The rising sun streaked through the curtain, bursts of light filtering into the room, making her skin glow. I didn't want this moment to end.

With one hand behind my head and the other resting comfortably on her perfect ass cheek, I had never been more content, even with our baby between us.

How I hadn't noticed the small bump or her aversion to alcohol and coffee was beyond me. I wanted to be mad. And if it had been anyone else, I would have left, spewing rage, but it was Logan.

The woman with electric green eyes that set my soul on fire and a smile that made my knees weak. There was something special about Logan. The moment she walked into that bar, everything changed. The second our eyes clashed, the minute I found out she could talk about beer, and the first time I heard her moan my name.

I didn't believe in soulmates until I saw Archer and Kenna find each other after years apart. As kids, we joked that she was his soulmate. That was where the nickname turtledove came from, but then, he left for college, and she disappeared a few years after and never came back—not until her Momma passed away.

Watching them rekindle their flame taught me that soulmates were real. I had to believe that Logan was mine.

We just understood each other in a way that words couldn't express.

She was carrying my baby, a life that we created with one reckless night. Glancing down at her peaceful face, freckles scattered across her cheekbones, long black lashes fanning her face, I knew could never be angry, and I couldn't leave her.

"Are you having second thoughts?" Her voice was huskier than normal in the morning. She didn't open her eyes, but her hand that was resting on my bare chest traced across my skin.

I cleared my throat before speaking. "About you and the baby?"

"Yea, about that." She was nervous. I saw her reaching for the chain around her neck, the one she never took off.

"I'll be honest with you—I didn't plan any of it. I wanted my career to be stable before ever lookin' for you."

She sat up, her dark hair covering her naked breasts, her eyes slitted. "You were going to look for me?"

"I knew after that night I wasn't done with you, Logan. I just wasn't ready for you."

"And you are now? Ready for me and a baby?" She was expecting horrible answers to hard questions.

Was I ready? Fuck no.

Would I get ready? Fuck yes.

I spent my life training; I could train for this, too. I would be a good boyfriend, fiancé, husband, and father. I would be the man she needed.

"I'm not gonna lie, Logan; I'm not ready." All the hope

drained from her face, and she jumped from the bed, picking up her robe from the ground and shoving her arms through it.

Following her, I grabbed her bicep and turned her around so I could see into her eyes. Tears were already slowly rolling down her cheeks.

"Woah, woah—don't shut down on me. You have to let me finish, sweetheart." I wiped the tears from her cheeks and cupped her face. "I'm not ready, but I *will* be ready. I have four months to do this right. Just give me a chance."

"I can't lean on you for four months only for you to decide when this baby is here that you don't want us," she cried, pulling her arm from my grasp. "You have to stop touching me. I can't think when you're holding me. I can't do what's best for me—for us." Her hands fell to her stomach, and I dropped to my knees.

I placed my hands over hers and looked into her big, green eyes. "I don't just want you, Logan; I need you. And I won't stop wanting or needing you until I die, and then, I'll probably still need you in the afterlife."

She was shaking her head, but she wasn't moving out of my grasp. It felt like a small win.

"This is crazy. We barely know each other. If it wasn't for this baby, we wouldn't even be here right now!" I didn't agree with her. Raising up, I kissed her round belly.

"I know you're the person I want to spend forever with. I know that my heart beats for you. I know that you make me happy. And Logan, I know that I would have found you if you didn't come for me." Big, fat tears were rolling down her cheeks. Her hands were still under mine, so she couldn't wipe them away.

"How do you know?" she croaked.

How could she not know?

"You're my soulmate, sweetheart. There's no ifs, ands, or buts about it. You were made for me, and I was made for you."

"What are we going to tell everyone?" She crouched so that we were at eye-level, and I saw the familiar panic clouding her eyes.

Cupping her face, I wiped away her tears and make sure to look straight into her hypnotizing eyes. "We don't have to tell them anythin' today. We can go to this weddin' and just be a couple in love. Nobody needs to know for another day." She nodded, but panic was still tensing her muscles.

"What are they going to think of me when they do find out? What if they see my bump with my dress? What if they find out today, and the news steals the show from your brother's wedding? Oh, my God, I can't go. I'll just stay here." She was rambling, her words mixing together.

"Deep breath, sweetheart. Inhale with me." She nodded but struggled to follow my actions. "And exhale. Do it a few times, okay?"

We repeated the simple routine until she was calm once again. "Nobody will be mad. Everyone in this family loves kids, and everyone—and I mean everyone—will be pleased that I'm ready to settle down." She nodded, her brows drawing together.

"But they all want you to settle down here, and I don't know about moving."

"Me neither. I don't even know what I'm having for breakfast, lunch, or dinner most days." She laughed a little. 'But we're in this together now. You and me against the world."

"I think I love you, Jaxon."

I softly smiled at her. "I think I love you, too, Logan."

117

CHAPTER 17
Logan

WE WERE GOING TO BE LATE. JAXON HAD SURPRISED ME last night, and again this morning, with his response to me and the baby. Never in my wildest dreams did I think he would want us.

Quickly braiding my hair back, I flattened my palms down the soft, navy dress. It hid my bump while enhancing my other features, and I was pleased with the way it softened my features.

Jax knocked on the bathroom door, reminding me we were ten minutes late already. Since he was part of the wedding party, we had to be early.

"Just one more minute." I squirted some of my favorite perfume on my neck, swiped some pink gloss on my lips, and then checked my hair one last time.

Stepping out of the bathroom, I wasn't expecting Jaxon to be leaning against the frame, looking ever-so-dashing in a black tux. He caught me as I crashed into him, and then, his beautiful, caramel eyes swept over me, darkening.

"Wow, sweetheart." He pressed the softest kiss to my cheek, his beard rubbing against my skin in the most delicious way.

"It hides the baby." I showed him, proud of the hours Scarlett and I spent searching.

"You shouldn't have to hide our baby." His hands cupped my belly as he stared into my eyes. "I don't need you to hide. I don't want you to hide either. Now that I know, I want the entire world to know, Logan."

If only he knew that one request for everyone to know would nearly break us.

* * *

AT THE RECEPTION a few hours later, I waited for Jaxon at our designated table, scrolling through Instagram while the family posed for pictures.

"Logan, where are you?" Kenna's southern drawl pulled me out of my daze, and suddenly, she was right in front of me. "Why aren't you with us?" She extended a hand to help me stand, and I wondered if she knew.

"Family pictures. Didn't think I should be there," I told her as she led me to where everyone was posing.

"Honey, you are family now. Come stand with your man and smile. We want you here." Her kindness was overwhelming, and I had to blink away tears. I wanted to tell her. I wanted to tell someone else that I was carrying his child, but I was scared of it ruining any chance of me being included in this beautiful family.

Jaxon spotted me immediately and walked over, pulling me into his arms and pressing a kiss to my temple. He then led me back to his spot, where he put me in front of him. "You're part of my family, Logan. You belong here with me," he whispered. Chills skated down my spine as his hands wrapped around my belly.

With him pulling the material tight on the dress, everyone would see, but he didn't care.

The photographer told us to smile. He complimented the bride and groom, who were glowing with happiness from what I could see out the corner of my eye.

"Oh, my God!" Brooklyn, who was to my right, squealed, and

I turned to look at her. Then, I saw exactly where her eyes were laser-focused. "You're pregnant!"

Everyone in the wedding party was looking at me now.

Jaxon's brothers immediately left their positions to tackle their youngest brother in congratulations, acting like teenage boys rather than grown men, their laughter infectious. The women quickly circled me.

"Congratulations, Logan!"

"Is it boy or girl?"

"How far along are you?"

"Are you gettin' married?"

The questions flew at me from all directions, but all I seemed to notice was the immense happiness coming from everyone. I was accepted in this family. I was wanted.

I'm going to be okay, Mom.

Jaxon was at my back again, and his arms wrapped around me. I stole a glance up at him, catching the biggest smile I'd ever seen on his face.

I made this beautiful man smile.

"We're pregnant," he tells everyone, like they didn't already know, and I sank into his hold, letting him answer the questions.

Would we get married?

I thought about my checklist for the hundredth time since finding out I was pregnant.

Find love. Check.

Get married.

Buy a house, preferably on the water, with lots of land for all the kids and dogs I want.

Rescue a dog.

Fall pregnant with the man of my dreams. Check.

Raise a beautiful family. Soon-to-be check.

I had the most important things checked off, and it didn't matter that they weren't in order. I found love in Jaxon. Sure, it was in the most unconventional way. I wasn't supposed to fall pregnant first, but didn't everything happen for a reason?

What would my mom say?

Did it really matter?

"Where are you, sweetheart?" Jaxon whispered, his lips brushing my ear, setting my skin on fire.

"Just thinking," I told him as I partially listened to the family gush about our news, like it was more exciting than the wedding we were here for. What was more interesting was the excitement coming from Carter when we just stole her entire show.

"Let me into that pretty mind of yours." Jaxon's focus was on me and nobody else.

"Just thinking about my list," I admitted, worried he might be tired of hearing about my damn list.

"What about it? Are you worried it's not goin' to come true?" There was a hint of fear in his voice, so I turned in his arms, looping my arms around his neck so I could look into his eyes.

"Not at all. It's all coming true. Not in order, but it's slowly becoming my reality," I told him, and he nodded in understanding, relaxing a little.

"I'll make it all come true, sweetheart. I will marry you. I will find you a house with lots of land and water. We will rescue a dog. And Logan, we are going to raise a beautiful family." My heart might just beat out of my chest from his words.

How was it possible for one man to be so perfect?

"You have my word that I will be checkin' every damn thin' off that list."

Jaxon Dexter was, in fact, a total swoon boat.

* * *

ON SUNDAY, we were supposed to go home, but Jaxon wanted to show me around his hometown, so we started the day in a tiny café called Mel's Café, where they had the best chocolate chip cookies I had ever tasted.

Then, he showed me where his older brother, Dante, worked training horses. Dante was busy giving Alice a lesson when we arrived but promised to give me some after the baby was born. He also told us about the trail rides he and Brook went on, which he swore made her fall in love with him.

We walked through Main Street, where Jaxon pointed out the places he used to hang with friends before leaving Honey Magnolia.

It was a quaint town that I had easily fallen in love with. We finished the night at his parents' house, where his mother showed me every baby picture she had of Jaxon and whipped up the best homemade mac and cheese I had ever eaten.

After dinner, we packed up the cabin, Jaxon loaded his truck, and I looked around the small space where my life had changed.

"What are you lookin' at?" he asked, coming to stand behind me, his arms wrapping around my middle.

"This place is where everything changed for the better." He chuckled, kissing my neck.

"Actually, sweetheart, that would be the hotel room." A giggle bubbled up my chest, and I slapped my hand over my mouth.

I was twenty-six years old—a grown woman giggling.

"I like it when you laugh," he whispered, his lips at my ear, nibbling on the sensitive skin.

"I like it when you kiss me." I turned in his arms.

"Like this?" He pecked my cheek. "Or like this?" He pressed his lips to mine, his teeth biting down on my bottom lip, begging for entrance, tongue swiping away at the sting.

When he pulled away, my fingers were curled into his hair, my chest rising and falling with shaky breaths. "That—like that," I whispered.

"Time to go home, sweetheart." He kissed my temple and then

led me to the truck, where we talked about our future for the next two hours, and then fell into his bed, completely and utterly exhausted and happy.

CHAPTER 18
Richard

"RICH, IF YOU DON'T CLEAN UP YOUR ACT, THE TEAM will have no choice but to switch you with another—better—player. My hands are tied right now," my agent reminded me about my exploding career.

I was nursing a hangover from the night before. One round of beers with a few friends turned into tequila shots and half-naked women. Now, there were headlines about what a player Pitcher Richard Balmer was, and the team owner was not pleased.

I had been warned a few years ago to keep my image clean. The team owner, my cousin, had told me to clean up my act. So, I had clung to the first good-looking girl I saw.

A young, hot, schoolteacher seemed like the perfect answer to all my problems. She'd been fun at first, fresh out of college, way too trusting, a great romp in the sheets, and the perfect, little girl-friend to clean up my image.

It had been fun until she started talking about the future. She didn't understand that I wasn't interested in ten years' time.

"I'll fix it." I closed my eyes and dragged a hand down my face, wishing I could pull the covers over my head and ignore my agent and all the other problems that he brought along with him.

"That's what you said last time. Now, that new pitcher, Jaxon Dexter, is starting at the game on Saturday."

You must be shitting me.

"I'll call Kyle," I say, referring to my cousin, the team owner, "and get him to talk to Coach."

"Kyle can't fix everything, Richard. His money is running out. There are rumors that he's going to be selling the team." I sat up, my eyes flying open. I look at my agent, who was dressed in a pair of joggers. He'd come prepared to get my ass out of bed and in the gym.

"What do you mean, running out of money?"

"News is spreading like wildfire. Nothing is confirmed, but your spot on that team, because of him, is not guaranteed anymore."

I hated not knowing the news first. I hated being the last to find out.

My phone buzzed from the bedside table, my best friend's name flashing on the screen. "It's Dylan. I have to take it," I told Liam, who crossed his arms with a scowl.

"Did you know Dexter has been shagging Logan?" Dylan's voice slurred through the speaker.

"What are you talking about?"

"Ramon just saw them at a restaurant all over each other."

"We broke up, Dylan. I don't care who she fucks anymore," I gritted out, tired of everyone talking to me about Logan.

"She's fucking pregnant, man. Could it be yours?"

Dropping the phone, I looked at Liam. This was either going to make or break my career.

I knew it wasn't not mine, but the public didn't know that, and if she was so far along in her pregnancy that Roman could tell, then she could have been cheating on me the whole time. Instead of me being the bad guy, I could be the victim.

I could spin everything in my favor. I could make everyone pity me and hate Jaxon, securing my spot on the team.

"Get me a news reporter now."

CHAPTER 19

Jaxon

INHALE.

Exhale.

My fingers tightened around the steering wheel as I drove into the small neighborhood, where Logan was staying with Scarlett.

Today, she invited me to her OBYGN appointment, where we were going to find out the gender of our baby.

I still couldn't wrap my mind around the fact that this perfect woman was carrying my child, and in just four short months, we would be parents.

My phone buzzed in the center console, and seeing my agent's name flash on the screen, I quickly answered the call.

"What's up, man?" I owed everything that I had to Bill. Because of him, I was here in Atlanta, playing for my dream team.

"Good news. It's not official yet, but Coach wants you to start at the game Saturday." He didn't waste time with pleasantries—never had—and it was one of the qualities I admired most about him.

"How did that happen? Did Balmer suddenly throw in the towel?" Bill cleared his throat, and I knew I wasn't going to like what came next.

"The team owner has run out of money, and after the game, the team will be up for bid." I pulled into the driveway of Scarlett's two-story home and shifted my truck into park.

"What does that mean for me?" Bill drew in a deep breath; he had come to know I didn't like beating around the bush.

"Balmer shouldn't be a problem for you after this game." So, I wasn't the only one who knew about his relationship with the team owner. I wondered how many other people knew about it as well.

"Thanks, Bill. I gotta run, but if you need me, I'm just a call away." Bill chuckled.

"Are the rumors true, Jax? You finally found someone to put up with your shit?"

I saw Logan exit the house, a bright smile greeting me with a little nervous wave. My heart squeezed in my chest. This woman. "You could say that. Catch ya later." I ended the call at his laughter and exited the truck, forcing myself not to run toward her.

I met her at the top step, wrapping my arms around her immediately and pecking her lips.

"Hey, cowboy," she greeted, her hands in my hair and her green eyes shining brighter than usual today.

"Hey, sweetheart. How's our little one doin' today?" I rested my hand between us and immediately felt movement.

"Excited to see their daddy," she said, looking up at me hesitantly. It was the first time she had called me that—the first time anyone ever had.

"I never thought I'd be a dad," I told her, pressing another kiss to her temple, inhaling her sweet scent.

"I never thought I'd be a mom either, but look at us." Pulling away, I raised a brow.

"Sweetheart, did you forget the part of your list where you raise a beautiful family?" She giggled and then slapped a hand over her mouth, cheeks flaming.

"After everything with Richard, I thought I was never going to find my person or even get to have a baby," she admitted as I helped her into the truck.

"I promise you that I will make everythin' on that list and more come true for you. I can't promise to do it right now, but with time, I will make it happen."

"Please don't make me cry. I just did my makeup." She swiped away at a stray tear and sniffled. "You're such a good man, Jax, and I just don't understand how I found you." She bit down on her bottom lip, and I grinned, wanting to kiss her more than I needed my next breath.

"I'll tell you how. You walked into that bar the night I won. You had my attention the moment you started talkin' about beer. And you owned my heart the first time you moaned my name, sweetheart. Once my position was settled with the Braves, I was comin' to find you." She flushed, her green eyes dilating with desire.

"And how were you going to find me? It's a big city, Dexter," she teased, saying my last name for the first time. And all I could imagine was calling her Mrs. Dexter.

"I was goin' to start at the bar, ask that old man you were pretty cozy with."

"And if he didn't give away my whereabouts?"

"I'd hire a private investigator." I shrugged, and she threw her head back, laughing.

"You are crazy."

"Crazy about you, sweetheart. Don't you ever forget that."

"We're going to be late for the appointment, Jax," she whispered, her fingers gripping my shirt, pulling me closer, even though she was asking me to move away.

"Are you nervous?" She shook her head, her fingers loosening their hold. "I am," I confessed. Her features softened.

"Don't be. We'll be there together." Nodding, I closed her door and jogged around the front of the truck to hop into the driver's seat.

* * *

AFTER SITTING in the waiting room with a few other anxious parents-to-be, we were finally brought back to a room where Logan was instructed to lift her top for the doctor to perform the ultrasound. She asked a lot of questions that Logan answered with fluency as I watched from my seat in the corner, hands on my knees. Finally, the doctor left, and an ultrasound technician came in, wheeling a machine.

"Alright, Dad. Do you want to come over here?" the technician addressed me, and I jumped up so fast, I saw stars. I trained my gaze on Logan, and her eyes twinkled with happiness. Every ounce of fear left my body.

Holding her hand, I watched the small screen. The technician pointed out the baby, and my heart stopped. Ten fingers. Ten toes. Two eyes. One nose. One mouth. One steady heartbeat.

Perfection.

"The doctor will be in shortly." She quickly left the room, and I stared at Logan, who was silently crying.

"Beautiful, huh?" she whispered, looking at the screen where our baby was frozen in a picture the technician took.

"I knew it was real. I mean, I can see that it's real. But wow— that just made it all the more real," I stuttered like a goddamn fool.

The doctor came in a few minutes later and immediately introduced herself to me. Then, she checked with Logan with another series of questions.

"Alright. Time for the fun part." She picked up the wand and brought it to Logan's belly, our baby flashing on the ultrasound machine once again. "Let's see what you're having." I didn't care if it was a boy or a girl. I thought maybe when the day finally came, I'd want a boy, but looking at Logan, at her perfect features, I wanted a little girl that looked just like her.

"Congratulations! You're having a boy!" Logan sighed, her

hand in mine tightening. My heart soared, my stomach dipped, and I fell to my knees.

I rested my chin on the bed, looking into Logan's tearful gaze. Completely overcome with emotion, a tear rolled down my cheek, and Logan caught it with her trembling fingers.

We were having a boy.

* * *

"Are you sure you want to come to the game tomorrow?" I asked Logan for the hundredth time. Since she found out I was starting and would more than likely play the entire game, she'd been dead-set on being there.

"Do you not want me to come or something?" she asked from the kitchen, pulling her head out of the fridge long enough to glare at me before tucking herself back into the fridge, muttering about a hot flash.

"It's just—are you sure you should be outside for all that time? And standin' with the baby?" I stood from the couch, switching off the football game I had been watching, and joined her in the kitchen.

"I was pregnant at the last one, Jaxon. You promised you wouldn't coddle me for another two months," she grumbled.

"Fine. Then just promise me you'll sit as much as possible." She stepped out of the fridge, closing it with a glare.

"I promise to sit whenever you aren't playing. How about that?" Rolling my eyes, I shook my head.

"Don't test me, Logan. I'll ask Coach to bench me if you want to play that game."

"You are a giant pain in the ass. Do you have any salt and vinegar chips?" She ignored me, searching through my pantry closet. Once she sees the giant blue bag of chips I knew she loved, she squealed. "Aw, you remembered!"

My anger deflated at her smile. She slid onto the barstool next to me and offered me some. "Not for me, sweetheart. Let's grab a movie before bed. I have to be up early."

An hour later, we were in bed, watching some old movie when my phone buzzed, and so did Logan's. We chose to ignore it, but then her phone buzzed repeatedly. "It's Scarlett. Let me grab it." She pressed the phone to her ear, and I watched her face drop, eyes going wide with fear.

"What's wrong?" I asked, gripping her forearm, but she was frozen as Scarlett screamed in her ear.

"Look at your phone," Logan finally managed to whisper.

I picked up my phone and saw numerous notifications—text messages from my agent and other teammates and numerous news articles. My eyes zeroed in on the headline of the article from the ESPN app.

Hot Shot Atlanta Braves' Ace, Jaxon Dexter, Has Baby With Rival's Ex.

CHAPTER 20

Logan

THROUGH BLURRED VISION, I READ THE TEXT FROM Scarlet.

> SCAR
>
> Logan!
>
> Logan!
>
> ANSWER ME DAMNIT!
>
> This has Richard's name written all over it.
>
> Did you know about the article?

The news article with a picture of me and Richard glared up at me. My hands immediately started to shake, the beginnings of an anxiety attack gripping my mind. I dropped the phone onto the soft comforter. When it fell, I just stared at my shaking fingers. The light from the TV cast an eerie glow over everything that I had once thought had been the perfect, romantic evening. Ruined.

Hot Shot Atlanta Braves' Ace, Jaxon Dexter, Has Baby With Rival's Ex.

The silence between me and Jaxon was too loud in his bedroom.

A glance toward him from the corner of my eye confirmed all my fears. His eyes were zeroed in on his phone, the screen illuminating his face. His eyes were set in a hard glare. He had seen it, too. He was mad at me.

The volume from the television was background noise compared to the drumming in my ears. Black spots danced in my vision while I tried my hardest to focus on breathing. I had to explain this to him—somehow. I had to tell him I didn't know about it. He had to know I would never sabotage his career.

I opened my mouth to speak, but only a strangled sob tore from my lips, the sound foreign and painful to my own ears. Words were impossible in my current state.

I shook my head, wishing I could find my control.

My lungs begged for air, my chest rising and falling too quickly, my heart beating too fast, the thrumming in my ears getting louder with every passing second.

In.

Out.

Inhale.

Exhale.

I can't breathe. I can't breathe. I can't breathe.

I clutched my chest with both hands and gasped for air. Jaxon's wide eyes were frantic when he looked at me. Quickly, he threw his phone off the bed, giving me his undivided attention. My fingers were ice-cold against my hot throat, but nothing relieved the burn from lack of oxygen.

Jaxon cradled my head, his hands ever so gentle, eyes betraying his calm movements. I gasped, my lungs burning, head spinning, speechless as I looked into his eyes and prayed he understood.

"Breathe, Logan. Breathe for me, sweetheart. Inhale. Exhale. You can do this. Breathe, baby."

I wanted to. I wanted to. I wanted to.

"Please, Logan," he begged, his voice shaking. It was unlike anything I'd ever heard before from him.

I wanted to scream at him that I couldn't control this. I wanted to tell him I loved him. I wanted to tell him that the article and whatever it contained wasn't true because I loved him.

"Don't close your eyes, Logan. Don't close your fucking eyes, sweetheart." I blinked slowly, everything unfocused except for the pain in his caramel eyes.

Is that a tear running down his cheek?

But the dark spots were getting bigger with every passing second, and it was too hard to keep my eyes open.

I'm sorry. I'm sorry. I'm sorry.

I love you, Jaxon.

* * *

"Just tell me how the baby is! I am her boyfriend and the father of our baby. That's my goddamn baby, and I need to know if they're goin' to be alright." Jaxon's anger could be heard from a mile away.

My throat ached, my head was pounding, and my entire body was heavy.

Where the hell am I?

"Sir, I believe you, but I can't release any information about the patient. You aren't supposed to even be in here," a female voice answered Jaxon's demand, and I heard him pacing. He scoffed, and I could just imagine him rolling his eyes.

"She is everythin'—her and my son are everythin' to me. I need to know they are goin' to be okay. Do you understand? Name your price; I'll pay anythin'." Jaxon was out of his damn mind.

I tried to move, to open my mouth, to twitch a finger—anything—but it was as though I was glued to the damn bed.

"Mr. Dexter, I will not be bribed, and you can be arrested for that."

"Ma'am, please. I'm beggin' here. Just tell me she's goin' to wake up." Jaxon's warm, callused hand gripped mine, and I tried to squeeze back.

The woman sighed, and I wished she'd just ease his fears. "She should be awake soon. Now quit pestering me." Her shoes squeaked as she left, and in the silence, I finally heard the machine beeping and could focus on the sterile smell of the room.

I hate hospitals.

"I'll fix this. I promise you, Logan. My agent is already workin' on it. I'll make it all go away. I know this wasn't you. I don't care if I lose my spot on the team over this. Nobody hurts my girl." His head dropped to the edge of the bed, his hair tickling my arm.

"What the hell happened?" Scarlett's loud voice echoed off the walls, and I cringed. I wished I could tell her to whisper.

"Anxiety attack," Jaxon grumbled, not paying her much attention.

"The baby?" she pressed, scraping a chair across the tile.

"Nurse won't tell me."

"Well, make them! You're Jaxon fucking Dexter. Don't you have a lot of money for a reason?" If I could move, I'd slap her.

"I already tried that. I was threatened with gettin' arrested."

"I hate this. I hate him for doing this to her. I hate everyone for hurting her." Scarlett sniffled. I hated when she cried; it was always ugly.

"How do you know it was him?" Jax questioned, his fingers tightening around my limp hand.

"Who else would do this? He wants you off the team, and he wants to hurt her for finding you. He cheated on her and used her to make his image look good, so he *wouldn't* get kicked off the team. Did she tell you that?"

Scarlett opening her damn big mouth.

"No, she didn't. I'm goin' to get him removed. I will fix this. She deserves better."

"She found you," Scarlett whispered, finally saying something worthwhile. I could kiss her. "You're all she needs. You and that baby."

It was silent for a long time. A nurse came by and checked my vitals, confirming that I should be awake soon, even though with every passing second, I was being lulled back to sleep.

"I love her," Jaxon mumbled, and immediately, I forced myself to listen.

"I know. Who wouldn't?" Scarlett whispered.

"I'm goin' to marry her," he spoke again, ignoring Scarlett's jab.

"Good. She wants something small—just your family and me, of course. Oh, and Matt. We can't forget him now." She was rambling like an idiot, but I loved her for it.

"And I'm going to find her a damn house with lots of land and a waterfront view."

"Ah, you've seen her list. She's had that list since her mom died, and every year on her mom's anniversary, she swears it'll never come true." I hated how much she was sharing with Jaxon.

I wished she'd shut her damn mouth and keep some of our secrets.

"I'm goin' to make that entire list come true, but first, I have to fix this mess and hope they let me play tomorrow."

The game!

"You're a good man, Jaxon, I'm glad she's knocked up with your baby. Otherwise, she would have been too chicken to come and find you again." Jaxon chuckled, and I swore I flushed about fifty shades of red.

"I can't wait to meet our boy," he said, and Scarlett gasped. I hadn't told her yet.

"It's a boy! Oh, I can't wait!" she squealed. I wanted to

smother her with a damn pillow. Didn't she know my head was pounding?

"Pretend to be excited when she tells you, okay?" Jaxon was nervous as he asked her, but she agreed and then started rattling on about all the cute names we should name our son.

* * *

WHEN I OPENED MY EYES, sunlight was streaming into the white room. Jaxon was asleep, his head about to roll off the side of the bed, his body slumped over in the hard, plastic chair.

Our hands were still intertwined together.

A nurse came in, and she checked everything, letting me know I had a major attack, and they had to sedate me. She went on about the baby and how he was perfect, and then, she glanced at Jaxon.

"That man sure does love you." I let my eyes drop to him—his messy hair, ashen skin, and rumpled clothes—and my heart soared.

"I know. He's very special."

She left, and I let my finger slide into his hair, massaging his scalp. He woke slowly, his eyes blinking and focusing. Then, he jolted upright.

"You're awake!" He rubbed the sleep out of his eye with one hand. I was pretty sure I fell completely in love with him in that moment.

"You've got practice, cowboy. You can't miss it. It's game day," I whispered. He kissed the palm of my hand that cupped his face.

"Nothin' is more important than you. How are you feelin'?" He reached for my face, tracing my lips, and I forgot how to speak.

What are words?

"Better," I finally managed, and he grinned.

"Good because I've got some people to burn today, and I need my girl healthy."

His girl.

"When can we go home? I hate it here." He nodded and stood. I immediately missed the loss of his touch as he stretched.

"Give me a few minutes to get you discharged. You're right. I hate this place, too. And you look better in my bed." He winked at my blush and sauntered out of the room, like our world didn't explode last night, like we didn't have enemies, like everything was just fine and dandy.

CHAPTER 21
Jaxon

"Be calm, Jaxon, I can see the steam coming out your ears, man." Bill was sitting beside me in the stuffy boardroom where we waited for Balmer, his agent, Coach, and the team owner.

"They can mess with me. They can do whatever they want to me, but not her. Not Logan," I told him, glaring at the door where I could hear Richard cracking a joke with his cousin.

"Do you want to be benched for the rest of the season, or do you want to be the Braves' ace? How you handle this situation will determine your future with this team," Bill whispered, looking between me and the papers he brought.

It was the article with Logan's face printed on it, a picture of her and Richard, and then one of me and her that some paparazzi had taken.

I clenched and unclenched my fists. Just an hour ago, I had dropped her off at my apartment, helped her shower, and gotten her to bed. She'd promised to be at the game later this afternoon with the help of Scarlett and Matt.

She'd also begged me to be levelheaded during this meeting.

"Be the bigger person, Jax. Don't threaten, don't scream—just let

him make an embarrassment of himself. You're the better man. You've always been." I let her words wash over me, willing them to calm my blind rage.

She was with me. Logan was all mine—she and that baby were my family. He couldn't take that from me—nobody could.

"If it was your wife, Bill? If someone had gone and dragged her reputation for his personal gain, your tellin' me you'd sit here and be calm?" My agent stiffened, looked towards the door, and then back at me.

"No, I wouldn't, but you don't have the luxury of losing your shit. Do you hear me? I want them to see that they can't affect you. If anything, he's the fool for losing Logan."

My phone buzzed on the table. I reached for it just as the door started to open slowly.

LOGAN

I love you, cowboy.

Sitting upright my attention first slid to my coach, who eyed me warily, and then, I scanned the rest of the group behind him. Richard was grinning like a fucking coyote with his agent behind him, nose buried in his phone. The team owner, Kyle, was behind him, eyes flitting around the room nervously like he was looking for something.

I was surprised to see another older man follow Kyle in, also dressed in a suit, hair neatly slicked back. A quick glance at Bill confirmed he wasn't expecting anyone else either.

Everyone took a seat, but Kyle remained standing, arms crossed. His short, usually neat hair, was ruffled, and purple bags beneath his eyes make them seem more sullen than the last time I saw him.

"Let's skip past the pleasantries. That article is a problem for me and for this team." He looked toward his cousin, who just shrugged.

"The problem is him. He shouldn't have gone after my girl."

Richard shrugged. Grinding my teeth, I gripped the edge of the wooden table, counting my breaths so I didn't jump across this damn table and strangle the son of a bitch.

"She wasn't yours the moment you cheated on her," I spat, barely holding myself back.

Kyle looked between me and Richard, and his brows raised. "And so, the story unfolds. Regardless of what happened that night, she is pregnant with your child, correct?" Kyle directed his attention to me, and for the first time, I notice that he wasn't favoring his cousin.

"Yes, she is. I understand this has put the team in a negative light, and I do apologize for the chain of events that led to that. But it wasn't her fault, and I didn't steal her from him. If you need me to leave, then I can."

Logan would be proud if she were here right now. She'd squeeze my hand or something, and damn if I didn't need that right about now.

The older man stood, slamming his palms down on the table. "Listen, I know I said I wouldn't say anything, but I can't sit here and watch talent walk out the door because your cousin, who has been on a slow decline for the last year, decided to kick up a storm."

He drew in a deep breath, straightened his suit jacket, and looked directly at me. "My name is Rick Stephen, and I am going to be the new team owner. I appreciate your dedication to not only this team but Ms. Shaw as well. You are exactly the kind of team member I want, and I will not let you leave this team."

I sat back in my seat, stunned. *That was unexpected.*

"Rick, let's discuss this privately," Kyle started, but Rick raised his hand. Kyle fell silent.

"I've listened to you. I've heard every excuse. This team is suffering because of you and your personal interests." Rick shot a glare at Richard, who hadn't opened his goddamn mouth. "The first *right* decision you made this season was recruiting Dexter, and

I won't lose him. Balmer, this will be your last game with the Atlanta Braves. I will not have any animosity on my team." He nodded at me and Bill and then exited the room.

* * *

"HE DID WHAT?" Logan screeched in my ear. Pulling the phone from my ear, I focused on my locker, checking my gear. Practice started in ten minutes, and I wanted her to know everything was okay.

"Don't wait for me today. Let Scarlett take you home. I'll shower and be right there; I promise."

"The doctor told you I was alright and so is our boy. I'm going to be there today, and you bet your damn ass I'll be waiting for you with the rest of the women." Grinning at the picture of her in my locker, my heart soared.

"I love you, sweetheart."

"More, cowboy. Now, go kick some ass. I'll be there later. Just look for the girl wearing your numbers. Wait—I bet there are a lot of girls wearing your shirt. Well, shit," she started to ramble, and my grin widened.

"Trust me, Logan, I'll find you. I'll always find you in a crowd. Plus, none of the other girls are carryin' my son."

* * *

AFTER THE GAME, I showered quickly and rushed out to get to my girl. Outside the locker room, I saw her, her black hair pulled back into a ponytail, my jersey pulled tight over her rounding belly. Scarlett was standing beside her, her arm linked with Logan, with Matt standing behind them.

Even though she was surrounded, it didn't stop Richard, who was a few feet in front of me, from charging at her. I pushed past fans and other players to get them.

"You fucking bitch! You told him everything! You weren't supposed to tell anyone about Kyle, yet you couldn't keep your mouth shut. You and I were together to clean up my image, yet you've ruined it!" He was screaming. Heads were turning in their direction. And my girl wasn't cowering back from him.

Her green eyes were slitted in a glare, and her cheeks were flushed, betraying her embarrassment of him for making a scene.

I dropped my bag to run faster and slid between him and her just as he raised his hand to push her. I absorbed it, standing my ground. Her small hands were at my back, gripping the fabric of my shirt.

"Get away from her," I gritted, but his anger only intensified.

"Oh, look here—the star of the game, Jaxon Dexter. Fucking bane of my existence. Stealing my position, my team, my girl— what next?" The rest of the team was slowly coming to stand at my side, but it did nothing to stop Richard's anger. "At least I had her first. When you fuck her next, just think—I've already been there!" I saw red just as Logan's hand slid around my torso, trying to hold me back.

"Don't do it. Don't—don't. Please don't!" she cried, her touch grounding me. I fought every cell in my body that wanted to knock this chump on his ass. She didn't deserve this.

She was so much better than his cruel words.

"You need to leave, Balmer," I told him, my hands clenched into fists at my sides. We were chest to chest, the scent of stale sweat wafting off him.

"Didn't know you let a bitch control your dick," he kept pushing, but Logan was wrapped around me, and if moved, I would only hurt her, our baby, and my future.

He wasn't worth it.

"Balmer, get your shit and get out of my stadium now!" Rick yelled from the entrance to the tunnel, where a few paparazzi were holding up cameras, and fans were recording with their phones.

We had made a big scene, but Balmer was the fool. I was just a man protecting his girl.

Two security guards stepped up behind Balmer and pulled him away as he spit at me, seething and still screaming his threats. I turned in Logan's arms, and she snaked her arms around my neck, her fingers sinking into my hair.

I cradled her face, taking in her perfect pink lips, flushed cheeks, and frantic eyes. "It's over. He's gone. I'm sorry. I'm sorry, sweetheart." I pressed a kiss to her temple just as the first sob escaped her chest.

I pressed her face into my chest as she began to cry. Her words were muffled, but her fingers tightened around me. So, I held her closer to my body, hiding her from the view of any cameras.

"Got your bag, man," Matt mumbled. I saw him standing behind Logan with Scarlett under his arm. She was crying, too, but her eyes were solely focused on her best friend.

I nodded at him in thanks before returning my focus to Logan.

"He won't hurt you again. He's gone, Logan. He's gone, baby." She craned her neck to look at me, and I saw the fear in her eyes slowly drain away to anger.

"I'm not scared of him; I was scared for you, Jaxon! I thought he was going to hurt you!" This beautiful woman. I didn't deserve her.

"I can handle a crazy like him." She shook her head.

"Your career—he was going to ruin it if you fought him. I didn't want to be the reason you lost your purpose." Sliding my fingers through her silky thick hair, I inhaled her sweet scent.

I then brushed my lips with hers. God, I needed her.

"*You* are my purpose, sweetheart. Not the game, not the sport. None of that matters if I don't have you. I would have gladly walked away today with my contract terminated if it meant protectin' you from him. Logan, you are everythin' I want and didn't know I needed. When are you goin' to understand that?"

I brushed away the warm tears rolling down her cheeks.

"I guess you'll have to keep reminding me, cowboy."

"How about every day?" Her brows drew together in confusion.

"Move in with me, sweetheart. Let's turn one of those empty bedrooms into a nursery for our son and move all your shit into my bedroom. Let's go to bed together every night and wake up together every mornin', where I'll remind you that you are my everythin'."

Scarlett squealed behind her and started clapping her hands. "I wish I had this on camera!"

Logan smiled and rolled her eyes. "You do know she'll be visiting all the time," she whispered, standing on her toes to press her lips to mine in a soft kiss.

"We can lock the door. I'll buy a deadbolt," I whispered, my lips brushing hers.

"As if that would ever keep me out," Scarlett scoffed.

"I'd love to move in with you, cowboy." I closed the small gap between our lips again just as the fans and my teammates burst into cheer around us.

I tuned them out and focused on the most beautiful woman in my arms. The one I was going to marry. The one I was going to buy a big house for. The one I was going to love for the rest of my life.

CHAPTER 22
Logan

Four Months Later

Getting into my car wasn't easy anymore with my protruding belly almost pressing against the steering wheel. I had to recline the seat and then struggled to reach the pedals. Clipping the seatbelt in, I started the car and checked my surroundings before pulling out of the grocery store parking lot. Tonight, I was going to make Jaxon a romantic dinner. His sister-in-law, Kenna, had told me his favorite meal, and I'd bought all the ingredients for it.

Merging into traffic, I noticed a big, white truck following my movements. I wouldn't normally think anything of it, except my gut was twisting with anxiety. A little on edge, I changed lanes, and the Tundra followed. Swallowing thickly and trying not to panic, I took the next exit to jump on the highway. The truck let another car between us, but my muscles were tight. The truck was definitely following me—just kept at a distance.

Reaching for my phone in my bag, I blindly patted around for it. Once the cold device was in my grasp, I called Jaxon.

"What's up, sweetheart?" His voice eased some of the panic clawing at my throat. Checking my rearview mirror, I saw the truck was now right on my bumper.

"J-Jax," I stuttered, pressing my foot harder on the accelerator and changing lanes again.

"What's wrong? Is it the baby?" There was panic in his voice now, and my heart raced, no longer calm.

"Someone is following me. I can't see through the windshield. It's—but maybe it's him..." I trailed off, remembering Richard's face when he'd been dragged away after his last game with the team.

"Where are you now?" There was a loud commotion in the background, deep voices asking him questions that fell silent quickly.

I told him my location and changed lanes again when he began to give me directions.

"Stay on the phone with me. How fast are you going?"

Glancing down at the digital speedometer, I cringed. "85, and he's on my rear. If I brake, he'll hit me hard." Jax's phone connected to his truck, and I heard his friends in the background.

"Don't panic. I'm comin', okay? I won't let anything happen to you, sweetheart. You're going to be safe. He won't hurt you ever again." His truck roared through the speaker as he accelerated.

I merged into the fast lane between two cars, where the white Tundra couldn't follow me. He roared past me and rolled down his window. Richard's crazed eyes gleamed at me. Sweat gathered at the back of my neck, and my fingers shook where they grasped the steering wheel.

"It's him. Oh, God, he's going to run me off the road, Jax!" Fear was ripping my throat apart, and I could no longer control the panic that was slowly seizing my body.

"Fuck. Be calm, Logan. Can you hear me? Listen to my voice. I'm not goin' to let him hurt you or my son." His truck revved loudly as he rushed to get to me.

My heart was racing, pounding so loudly that I couldn't hear him over the blood rushing in my ears. His voice wasn't calming me. All I could see was my increasing speed and Richard's angry expression.

"What do I do?" I whispered, slowing down when the semi in front of me suddenly slammed on the brakes, traffic coming to a standstill. Richard was next to me, boxing me in. And now, he was opening his door and getting out.

"I'm here." I couldn't see Jaxon's F-150, but suddenly, he was at my door, trying to yank it open. I shakily unlocked the door and unclipped my safety belt, relief flooding my veins at the sight of him. He pulled me into his arms, pressing a kiss to my forehead. "He won't hurt you, Logan. The boys are back there. Go with them."

Luke, Jax's best friend, was standing there at Jaxon's back, arms crossed over his chest, glaring at Richard over the roof of my sedan. Jax pushed me toward Luke, and I tripped over my own feet, straight into him.

Luke's hand gripped my forearms, pulling me in front of him as he walked us back a few cars to Jaxon's black F-150. I slid into the backseat with two of the Braves players Jax had befriended.

"Hey, boys." My voice shook when I spoke, but they smiled.

"Hey, Logan. Sorry about that dick, but you don't have to worry. We're here now. You're safe with us," Luke said from the front seat where he was gripping the steering wheel.

I watched through the windshield as Richard raised his hands up and pointed at the truck where I was sitting, rage coming off him in waves. I didn't know this side of him. Never once had he shown an ounce of anger to me in all the time that we dated. This side of him was terrifying.

"He's going to hurt, Jax," I whispered, biting my nails worriedly.

"Cops should be here any minute. We called them on the way," one of the guys beside me spoke up. I forgot his name, but in this moment, it didn't matter because he smiled softly. "Everything is going to be okay, Logan," he assured me. Everyone kept trying to assure me, but nothing felt okay.

True to his word though, a cruiser pulled up, red and blue light flashing. The officers immediately restrained Richard, who had shoved Jaxon up against my car.

They took my statement, and then Jax demanded a restraining order to keep Richard away, especially with our little boy due any day.

An hour later, Jax was driving me home in my car, and Luke was behind us in the F-150.

"How come Luke is here?" I asked, playing with the hem of my shirt, trying to find any distraction because the silence in the car was killing me.

"Came to visit," Jax grunted, his body stiff, both hands on the steering wheel. "Why weren't you at home? You know you shouldn't be drivin'."

I glanced out the window at the city. The buildings hid the setting sun, and I wished we were anywhere but here. He mentioned going to visit his family, but with the baby due so soon, we hadn't really had a chance to go back, and he didn't want us to be so far from my doctor in case the baby came and there were complications.

This man was always worried about something going wrong.

"I spoke with Kenna earlier and wanted to make your favorite dinner. I was getting groceries." His body softened, and he placed a hand on my bouncing knee.

"You still up to cooking lasagna after all that?" There was a small grin replacing the frown that had been pulling his lips down.

"Depends on if you're up to helping and giving me a foot rub."

He cracked a grin. "Oh, that can be arranged, sweetheart. I'll do anythin' for you; you know that."

* * *

EVERYTHING WAS READY.

We'd painted the room a soft blue and decorated it with too many tiny baseball signs to count on one hand. Jaxon had found a giant mitt for a rocking chair, and even had a sign made with our son's name on it, which was hanging above the crib.

I spent hours with Scarlett in every baby store, buying all the cutest clothes, stocking up on diapers, and more things than I could ever possibly need.

Jax and I packed my bag two weeks ago, and then, we packed the baby's bag. Everything was waiting by the door for a quick grab when the time came.

We'd debated on his name for weeks, throwing random ideas around until suddenly, one day, it all just clicked.

Everything was ready—except me.

Pacing the apartment frantically, I rubbed my swollen belly and willed the nerves to leave. Thousands of women gave birth every day, every hour. Surely, I could do this, too.

Is it normal to be having an anxiety attack every time I think about pushing this baby out?

Jaxon came through the front door, sweat dripping down his flushed face, his dark hair longer than when we first met, and his beard thicker, too. God, I loved this man.

His caramel eyes latched onto mine, and he smirked. "Are you freakin' out again, sweetheart?" he teased, closing the distance between us with three large steps. His tan, calloused hands latched onto my waist. He flexed his fingers, each one setting a part of me on fire.

"Maybe a little," I whispered, looking up at him through my dark lashes.

"Come have a shower with me, and I'll get you nice and relaxed." He grinned, knowing exactly how much I had been loving our showers. There were so many spots I couldn't reach anymore...but Jax could.

"Tempting, but you go on. I'll wait for you in bed." We'd both been trying to get as much sleep as possible, knowing any day now, we'd be begging for these days to come back.

"Go rest, sweetheart. I love you." He kissed my nose and pulled away, leaving me in the middle of our home, completely and utterly in love.

He joined me not long after in bed and brought me impossibly close, his arms wrapped around me, big hands palming my belly, my back to his warm chest.

"We're having a baby, Jax," I whispered, closing my eyes.

"We are, sweetheart." He chuckled, lulling me to sleep.

A sharp pain woke me hours later, and I struggled to sit up, his heavy arm weighing me down. "Jax, wake up. Wake up!" I shoved him, and he bolted upright, eyes wide in alarm.

"What? I'm awake," he groggily slurred.

"It's time. He's coming!"

* * *

"HE'S PERFECT, LOGAN," Jax whispered, cradling our tiny son in his big arms. "I can't believe we made him." Jax only had eyes for Kane, and I couldn't blame him. He was precious.

"Me neither," I tiredly whispered, wishing more than anything I could record this moment—our first time together as a new family. I wished I could capture Jax's face, but looking at him now, seeing that smile, and the way his eyes softened, I didn't think I would ever forget this anyway.

Jax came over and sat on the edge of the bed so I could look at Kane. After twelve hours of labor, I could barely even lift my arms, but Jaxon did it for me, holding him out in his strong arms so I could admire our beautiful sone. Kane had my dark hair, but he had his daddy's nose and mouth.

A nurse came in, holding a clipboard. "Alright, Mom. Time for the first feed. Do you want to breastfeed or use formula?"

I'd done enough research to know that breastfeeding was the

best route, but I couldn't imagine finding the strength to hold him.

Times like this, I longed for my mother. She would know what to do.

Jaxon also knew what route I wanted to go, so he spoke to the nurse, and she nodded, jotting down some notes.

"Why don't you help Mom here and hold him like this." She helps me unbutton the stiff gown and propped me up. Jax held Kane, and after a few attempts, Kane was suckling with his father supporting him.

"He's doing it!" I whispered in amazement, watching his sweet face as he softly suckled, making the tiniest moans of enjoyment.

"I love you, Logan. Thank you for givin' me this." I looked up at Jax. Tears were welling in his eyes as they shifted between me and his son. "I am such a lucky man."

Using the only ounce of strength I had, I raised my hand and rested it on his arm. "I couldn't do any of this without you. Thank you for being my strength, for helping me through the last few months, for holding our son to my breast when I'm too weak. We are just as lucky to have you."

He pressed the softest kiss to my temple. "I am so proud of you. I know you wish your mom was here, and I'm sorry I can't make that happen. But I'm here, Logan, and I promise I'm not goin' anywhere. I'm kinda crazy about you." He grinned—that teasing grin I had come to love—and if I didn't already love him with my entire heart, I would now.

Once Kane had enough, the nurse taught Jax how to burp him, and I stifled giggles while watching my big husband hold our tiny little boy on his shoulder and tap his back until he burped. The grin that took over his tired face was worth all the pain.

"That was a big one! How does that feel, buddy?" Jax cooed to our son, lowering his deep, husky voice to speak to the infant.

I wanted to spend the rest of my life loving this man.

"Hey, sweetheart, you think you'll want another one?" Jax asked once he'd rocked Kane to sleep. "So far, he's a piece of cake."

"Ask me again in a week," I whispered, fighting my own exhaustion.

"Even if he turns into a terror, will you want another one with me?" He hesitated on the question, but I couldn't get my eyes to open, so I blindly reached for his hand.

"I want everything with you, Jax." He intertwined our hands, and everything was just right.

"Good because I want three more." He chuckled, and by some miracle, my eyes flew open.

"Three?!"

His grin was priceless, and even if he wasn't so goddamn sinfully handsome, I'd probably still give him as many damn kids as he wanted.

"I need a little girl that looks like you and a few more boys to keep her safe."

"You're crazy, Dexter." I let my eyes fall shut again.

"We've already established that. Now, sleep, my beautiful girl, because this little man is a Dexter, and we don't sleep much."

Our little Kane Dexter.

I wanted to be a Dexter, too.

Epilogue

JAXON

Six Months Later

Kane suckled loudly on the bottle of breast milk I was feeding him. The sun had barely risen, and he was wide awake, his momma's eyes shining up at me with more love and adoration than I deserved.

"You're a good boy, Kane. Drink up, buddy," I whisper softly, hoping to keep this short so I could climb back into bed with Logan and catch another hour of sleep before morning drills.

He'd been an easy baby. At least, that was what everyone said. And every time they did, I watched Logan stiffen, her eyes turn to slits, and she'd shake her head. The first three months had, in fact, not been easy.

But from what I had heard, it never was. At least we figured out getting him to sleep through the night. We were both struggling with taking turns at night and then trying to cope with our days.

After he finished the bottle Logan had prepared for him last night, I held him upright on my knee and gently patted his back, rubbing out three loud belches before rocking him back to sleep. Never thought I'd sing until we learned that he liked my terrible voice, so now, I sang *only* for him, and it soothed him straight to sleep every time within minutes.

After laying him in his crib, I tiptoed out of the room and crept into the main bedroom, where Logan was just getting out of bed.

"Not so fast." I jumped into the bed, pulling her to my chest.

"I need to feed Kane," she groggily mumbled, cheek on my chest.

"Already done, sweetheart. Go back to sleep."

"Mmh. Okay. You're the best dad," she whispered, falling back asleep, her soft breaths brushing against my bare chest.

And she was the best mom. I knew she had been worried about knowing what to do with our son, but like everything else she did, she was a natural. Plus, if he was anything like me, he had to be smitten with her.

She was perfection.

Closing my own eyes, time flew by too quickly, and then my alarm was going off, reminding me about the spring morning drills. Logan was grumbling about it being too early.

Kane wouldn't wake for another hour or two, so I slipped from the bed and headed into the bathroom, wishing I could spend the morning in bed with Logan, making another baby.

* * *

SITTING in my truck after practice, still trying to catch my breath, Logan sent me a picture of her and Kane, making my heart ache in a way I didn't know was possible.

And then, my brother's ugly mug filled the screen, the phone vibrating with the incoming call.

"You're annoyingly on time," I grunted at Archer, who chuckled.

"You still comin' down this weekend to show her the house?" he asked, mentioning the house I'd bought for me and Logan a month ago after Archer sent me pictures. It filled every goddamn requirement we had.

After this season, I would be retiring and moving back to Honey Magnolia, where Archer had already arranged for me to become the coach of the high school baseball team. I was also planning on starting a little league for Kane so he could one day join if he loved the sport.

"Yeah. What kind of shape is the place in? Do I need to bring tools?" The listing's pictures were beautiful, but I hadn't seen the house in person and didn't want to be blindsided.

"Looks better than the pictures, man. Kenna wants to host dinner on Saturday night after you show her the place, and Mom already got the cabin ready for you all."

Wiping a hand down my face, I hadn't thought about where Kane was going to sleep in the one-bedroom cabin.

"She also offered to take Kane for the night. So did Carter, Brooklyn, and Kenna." Archer chuckled.

"Seems like he's goin' to be a ladies' man this weekend," I joked, thinking back to everyone's reactions when they came to visit us in the hospital just six months ago, and then again how everyone fussed over him at Thanksgiving and Christmas.

"The women in this family loves babies—almost like we don't give them enough." He snorted, speaking of his pregnant wife.

"I thought I didn't want kids," I told him, shifting the truck into gear so I could get home to my family.

"And then, you met her, and now, you want a whole herd of Jaxons and Logans, right? Welcome to the damn club." Archer hit the nail right on the head.

"Somethin' like that," I agreed, thinking about all the children I wanted to have with Logan. At least two more—though I was hoping I could get her to agree to three. I grew up with three brothers, and it was the perfect number, but seeing as Logan was an only child, I wasn't sure if she would be easily convinced.

"You think she's gonna like the house?" he asked. I thought

back to her three requirements on that list I was determined to check off.

"She wanted enough land for a dog to run free, a water view, and a place to raise a family. If it has those things, then she'll love it."

"When you gettin' the dog?" He snorted again.

"After we move in. Don't have room for one now." I thought about the already crowded penthouse. Most days, I came home to Scarlett lounging in front of my TV, eating my food while holding my son.

That woman needed to have her own kid and eat her own damn food.

"Alright. See you Saturday. I'll try to keep the hounds at bay on Friday, but no promises. Mom is so excited to have all of us back in the same town again. It's good to see her so happy."

Logan barely spoke about her mom, other than how hard her absence was from her life and these milestone moments, so it made me want to be closer to mine before it was too late. Logan often urged me to spend more time with my family.

"See you Saturday, Archie. Say hi to Kenna for me." He mumbled his agreement and ended the call. A few minutes later, I was pulling into the parking garage below my building.

Now, I just had to convince Logan to go to Honey Magnolia for the weekend.

* * *

LOGAN

Kane loved sleeping in his car seat. Every time we put him in it, he went straight to sleep without any fuss. Jax had been oddly silent on the ride over to Honey Magnolia, his fingers drumming against the leather steering wheel. He softly hummed the tune to the old country song under his breath, careful not to wake Kane.

"Why the sudden trip?" I asked for the tenth time since he asked if we could go visit his family earlier this week.

"Look, they call me every day, and I just couldn't say no anymore." I caught the slightest grin tugging at his lips.

"Calling about Kane?" I asked, knowing Kane's grandma sure did love him a lot more than I ever expected.

"And us, of course, but yeah, mostly him. Oh, and Kenna's pregnant, so they wanted to have an announcement dinner Saturday night."

"Aw! I'm so happy for them! Were you supposed to tell me if there's going to be a dinner?" I asked, but he just shrugged.

"They know better than to ask me to keep secrets."

He really could not keep a secret. But it was another thing I loved about him.

An hour later, we rolled into Honey Magnolia. The big Magnolia trees were in full bloom for the spring. I really loved it here. It was quiet, peaceful, and possibly the perfect place to raise Kane with the rest of Jax's family here. But I'd been worried about bringing it up because it would likely be the end of his baseball career.

I didn't want to be the reason he gave up something he loved so much, so I left the ball in his field.

"Everyone's offered to take him for the night if you want to have a break," he mentioned as we pulled up in front of the cozy cabin he'd first brought me to last year. It was the place I'd told him I was pregnant for the first time, and the same place I'd tell him again.

He didn't know that I was six weeks pregnant with our second child.

The whole idea of it all freaked me out. We were so far from my freaking ten-year plan—still no ring on my finger, no home to fill with kids, and no dog, but I had the man I was hopelessly in love with, so what else did I need?

"And there's my mother now," he groaned, sliding a hand

through his dark hair. "Tell me now if I must put my foot down," he whispered, and I shook my head with laughter.

"Let him go. It's just one night, and we'll be right here if anything goes wrong. We can just run over." His eyes went wide with the realization that I was the one letting him go, but he didn't have a chance to say anything because his mother was already slowly opening Kane's door and sighing at how cute he was.

"You make the cutest babies," she sighed, watching his sleeping face.

We really did.

"Thanks, Mom. I get it that you love my son, but what about me?" Jax joked, getting out of the car and hugging his mother. I rounded the truck, and she also pulled me in for a squeeze, warming my heart, like she always knew how to do.

She'd taken me in as one of her kids, filling a hole that had been gaping open for far too long in my chest.

"I've missed you both so much! Now, about my grandson. Can I take him for the night—give you two some time to make me another one?" She laughed, and Jaxon cringed.

"Jeez, Ma. What the hell?" he exclaimed, waking Kane.

I unbuckled Kane from his car seat, kissing his chubby cheeks before handing him over to grandma, who squealed with delight.

"He's all yours. Bottles are in the bag, and he goes to bed at about nine at night and wakes up at sunrise." She slung his bag over her shoulder and cooed at him.

"We're goin' to have so much fun, aren't we, Kane? Just wait until Grandpappy sees how big you've gotten." She waved at us over her shoulder as she left, hopping onto a golf cart and slowly driving back to her house.

"When did she get that?" I asked, referencing the new golf cart.

"Dad got it for her for her birthday. She uses it to go visit Archer and check everything on the ranch." I nodded, helping him bring our bags into the small cabin.

"Since it's just us tonight, how about pizza and a movie?" I asked, and he grinned.

"We don't get delivery out here, but I'll go into town and get a half cheese and half Hawaiian. Shouldn't take me more than thirty minutes. Just enough time for you to have a bath and wait for me in those sexy pajamas I saw you pack." He winked on his way out.

Thirty minutes later, I was waiting for him in my new sexy pajamas on the couch with a movie waiting to be played.

"You look edible," Jaxon groaned, walking into the house and setting the pizza down on the coffee table before bending down and pecking me on the lips. "I'll be five minutes." He took off running, chucking his clothes as he went. The shower ran for two minutes before he was running back to me in my favorite pair of gray sweatpants.

We devoured the pizza, and then called his mom to check on Kane before settling in for the movie. An hour in, his lips were trailing up my jaw, his tongue tracing a pattern up to my ear, where he nibbled on my lobe.

"Jax," I moaned, closing my eyes and arching my head back.

"Let's make another baby, Logan," he whispered in my ear. My stomach somersaulted.

"About that," I started, pulling back to look into his eyes. I saw it the second he sensed my hesitation.

"You don't want anymore?" I shook my head quickly, and he paused, his hands encircling my wrists, his lips dangerously close to my chest.

"I'm already pregnant, Jaxon." He threw his head back and laughed before falling silent and kissing me speechless.

"You amaze me every fuckin' day, Logan. How far along are you?"

"Six weeks, so don't go telling everyone just yet." He rolled his eyes and sighed.

"You know I hate secrets."

"And I know just how to make you forget," I teased, taking off my top. His eyes darkened with desire.

"Yes, you do, sweetheart. Yes, you do."

* * *

THE NEXT MORNING, Jaxon was pulling me out of bed and urging me to shower so we could somewhere.

"I'm tired and sore. Can't it wait?" I asked leaning against him in the shower as he soaped up my body.

"Nope, it can't, and if you don't help me, I'm going to make you sorer." My body erupted in flames of desire for him. He couldn't threaten me with sex.

Ten minutes later, he was helping me into the truck, and we were zooming toward his parents' house, and then past it.

"What about Kane?" I asked, looking out the window.

"This is a surprise for us, sweetheart," he told me. Reaching over, he linked our hands together on my leg. I watched the scenery fly by, and then suddenly, we were slowing down and turning onto a secluded drive that wound up to a big, country home with a white, wrap-around porch.

"What is this place, Jax?" I asked just as he put the truck into park and shut it off.

He pulled out a familiar, crumpled-up piece of paper from his pocket. It was my list. My ten-year checklist. He handed it to me, and I saw two new check marks.

Find love. Check

Get married.

Buy a house, preferably on the water, with lots of land for all the kids and dogs I want. Check.

Rescue a dog.

Fall pregnant with the man of my dreams. Check.

Raise a beautiful family. Check.

I looked at him through my blurry vision, and he nodded, his lips pulling into a soft smile. "It's ours. A house on the water with lots of land," he whispered, his voice full of more emotion than I could handle.

Tears rolled down my cheeks. God, this beautiful man.

"I told you I'd check everythin' off that list slowly. Next, I'm puttin' a damn ring on your finger, Logan. You can't keep havin' my babies without bein' my wife."

I choked on a cry and a short laugh.

"I love you more than words could ever describe," I told him, taking his hand and pressing it to my shaking lips.

"Come look at our home, sweetheart. Look at the place we are goin' to raise our beautiful family." He helped me out of the truck and stood behind me, his arms wrapping around my body, holding me to him. "Can you see it?"

"See what?" I whispered, trying to take everything in. The big house, porch, acres of land, water view—he actually did it.

"In that tree," he pointed toward a big, old tree, and I follow his hand, "I'm going to hang a tire swing for the kids. Over there," he pointed again, "I'm going to make a field to play whatever sport the kids want. And over there," he pointed in yet another direction, "the dogs are going to chase the kids. Tell me you can see it, sweetheart?"

I nodded. "I see it, Jax. I see it!" I exclaimed, tears running down my cheeks. I saw my future with him clear as day.

Turning me in his arms, he wiped at my tears with his fingers and then kissed the wetness away with his soft lips. Tilting my head up, I pressed my lips to his, and for once, I prayed that I stole his breath away, too.

THE END

I HOPE YOU ENJOYED ALWAYS MY COMFORT! Want a peek into Logan and Jaxon's future? Subscribe to my mailing list and you'll get instant access to an exclusive bonus scene!

Thank You

Thank you for reading *Always My Comfort,* a small town, secret baby romance. I hope you enjoyed your adventure with Jaxon and Logan! Please consider leaving a review on Amazon/Goodreads! They really help authors like me SO MUCH!!!

Start The Series

Always My Hero

Everyone knew the Dexter brothers. In school, they were royalty, and their kingdom was the football field, the crowd their subjects.

While most people in our small town stayed and went to the community college nearby, the Dexter brothers all left, each with a full-ride football scholarship to play at some hotshot university on the other side of the country.

I left too, but I only went one state away, far enough away to get out of the small town I grew up in.

But now, ten years later, I was back, feeling like the same shy, nervous, eighteen-year-old girl I was when I left.

All at once, it felt like everything and nothing had changed.

But Archer Dexter was back, dreams of becoming a famous NFL player crushed because of a career-ending injury.

He's now the town mechanic and tow-truck driver.

And when my car breaks down, he's my only hope of getting out of this wretched town that I should have never come back to.

Acknowledgments

Mom,

I wrote this book after we spent a week in Vegas learning everything we could about an industry we did not understand. You push me to be better every single day, and without you this book would not be what it is today.

Thank you always believing that I was meant to be a writer. Thank you for pushing me reach goals I thought were unattainable. Thank you for being a constant crutch in any situation I'm in.

This book, this series, these characters were made with love, and constant unwavering support from my family.

Also by Taylor Jade

Printed in Great Britain
by Amazon